Contents

I0519641

Introduction

The author, Phil Rowe, wrote a synopsis of his works (see below), after completing most of the novels he had intended to write. He had several reasons for designating his novels by different colors, but one, 'Relax Your Mind', seemed particularly appropriate. If you end up reading all of Phil Rowe's works you will want to look up the mellow yellow line too, and you will want to relax your mind.

When the light turns green
You put your foot on the gasoline
Sometimes you have to relax your mind
Relax your mind

When the light turns red
Put your foot on the brakes instead
Sometimes you have to relax your mind
Relax your mind

When the light turns blue
My, oh, my, what are you going to do?
Sometimes you have to relax your mind
Relax your mind

Synopsis by Phil Rowe

Once upon a time, actually in the early 60's, when Dick was in the Army, he had some adventures with his true love, Karen, a wonderful violist, and he wrote a novella which dealt in some "large metaphoric way" with those adventures—or at least with what he took to be the principal issues—concluding that he had a lot to learn. That was the Green Book, first of this series.

Then he left the Army and came to Rutgers, as a graduate student in English. His first year, he lived at Welton Street in New Brunswick with Bill, and Mike, and others. The following Spring, he bought a motorcycle, and in the summer lived with Al and Steve and Mike at Oak Street, where he thought a lot about life and art, and Karen (who was in Aspen, Colorado that summer, though she planned to winter in New Haven where she was a graduate student—they had never quite patched things up, you see), and he also thought more than a little about Steve's girlfriend (whose name was also Karen, and whose hair was red), because she was beautiful and strikingly like a character he had invented (he thought) for the Green Book. Hence, Karen-Of-The-Red-Hair. There were a few other Karens, too; most prominently, Karen-Blue-Eyes; who was a friend of Mike's, and then of Al's.

Well, it was a summer full of doings and happenings, all set forth in fine style, in the so-called Red Book, so that you can read all about it. And Dick had just about decided to "get involved", when he decided not to. And then Karen returned from Aspen, and he took her for a motorcycle ride on Labor Day, and they crashed, and she wound up with stitches in her head, and he was so scraped up inside and out that he was swathed in bandages, had a funny dream, and stuttered. That, more or less, is the time spanned by the Red Book, and roughly what happened to Dick during that time.

The Red Book begins with a scene (which, by chronology, is really its last scene, though it is not repeated) which tells you about a night in Highland Park (where Dick came to live after that summer), a funny prank Dick played on some of his roommates (a musical beds sort of thing), and how they acquired a puppy named Blue. The Blue book carries the events forward in time from that night on, for a couple of months more. But since Dick and some of his friends have funny ideas about time (which we won't go into here), that's not all, by a long shot.

The current Blue book was originally intended to be the first of two parts. But it is necessary to think of it that way only if you count the Green Book as a whole book. If you see the Green Book (Dick's novella) as an overture, or haven't read it, or don't like it, or can't remember it—then really the first Blue Book ought to be the Red Book, and the one we've been calling Red ought to be Green. But that's silly, of course, because if that's how things are, then the Blue Book is a Red-Blue Book, or Purple—which is a royal pain, and carrying whimsy too far. So, call the Blue Book the Middle Book, if you will, which describes it pretty well, since there's only one more coming after this, and only one New Brunswick book before it.

The Middle Book consists of three parts. Its official temporary title is, 'Tailgates and Substitutes' which derives from these lines:

> *Buy me a flute*
>
> *And a gun that shoots*
>
> *Tailgates and substitutes*
>
> *Strap yourself to the tree with roots*
>
> *You ain't goin nowhere*

Bob Dylan wrote those lines. Who wrote these books, is something of a puzzle, but for now I'll take the overall blame.

Philip Rowe

Editor's note—the final book never got written or was lost or the editor didn't notice when the first Blue Book merged into the second Blue Book. Well, it's not important anyway. Credits are important though, so take note. Phil was a fan of the blues, so it's no surprise that he quotes Dave Van Ronk songs and took the title line 'I'm an educated man' and other key lines from "Born about Six Thousand Years Ago". "Relax Your Mind"—originally (H. Ledbetter, 1949 Leadbelly), though the blue line is hard to trace exactly.

Norfolk Connecticut

Norfolk Connecticut is a fairy-tale place where Yale University used to conduct a summer-school for music and art. The town is one of those small pastoral towns one comes to expect in the hills of New England. And though the grass and trees and streams of Norfolk are picturesque as they should be, were it not for the summer-school one might feel the oppression that characterizes so many of those towns—the sense that years of quaint beauty have inbred, that the grass is green from habit and the trees magnificent from a duty too obvious too long to be questioned. The folk of the town are as unfriendly as in any of these towns, and the young gangsters outside the Drugstore are of a type.

Yet there is—or was (for I have not returned for many years) —the summer-school, the half a hundred young artists who stroll and paint and sketch. They freshen the tired scenery which is their special property. They infuse it with the joy that is also their own. And where they drink their wine, love, quarrel, and discuss—there they quicken the landscape.

It is easy to be fanciful about them, to romanticize their neuroses and forget the personal trivial tragedies which attend all such inter-mixtures. But there is a contrast to define their joy—the half a hundred musicians, the more serious students, the awkward and (often) unlovely ones, the people who have spent their childhood practising. There is no need to labor the contrast or its reasons. There is more at stake for the musicians. There is less finality in the judging of a canvas than in that of a performance. The artists can relax in their failures. This is not to say that they do so—more, perhaps, that they could if they chose. Many of them have long ago ceased to worry about their place in society, and I suspect that musicians never stop worrying. It is a queer life, this art which is performances, and the musicians at Norfolk do not seem to live it with much joy. The blending and contrasting of these two groups, their teachers, and their friends at times exceeds the triviality it really is. Confined by the small town and interlocked by the many little paths and trails, the school—broadly—could come to be the setting of choice for any author.

I am neither a musician nor an artist. I came to Norfolk as a friend of a musician, who, I should say, was not awkward or unlovely. Her name was Karen, and, as I recall it, I loved her very much. I came to see and be with her, and to observe this fairy-tale place.

So, often while I was there the intrigues and complications of the people around me impelled me to begin stories about them and the school. Definition seemed so easy while I was there. But it was only the setting that forced my interest. As I would begin a story I would realize the triteness of my inspiration. For here were the same ordinary sordid and sentimental collisions of people. That the people were extra-ordinary made their infidelities, their grand passions, the fights, the illnesses no less ludicrous. Artists and musicians both—once you had cut through a few generalized distinctions—were conducting the ordinary business of living, and only the grass and trees created the illusion that here one could grasp some central truth about people. That—some central truth—was, I confess, what I wanted to write in those long-ago days. I was not then content to chronicle the ordinary business of living by extraordinary people. Oh, I hardly knew what it was I wanted to write of—but something, no doubt, of the elemental. The fundamental surrounded me and I groped for myth.

Much happened to me that summer. Against my observer's will I too entered into the passions of my community. In the process I learned truths no author can ever write; for they are as ludicrous and trivial as the grandest of human struggle. I suspect—though I have less arrogance about such conclusions now—that if the secrets of life so sought for by young authors exist at all, it is in the bitter quarrel over a spilled ashtray or a ping-pong point that they may be found. I am not the first author to note that all lovers use a similar vocabulary of quarrel, and that the only difference in the quarrels of the very intelligent lies in the embarrassment which accompanies each cliché; I am only the first to say this of the Yale summer-school at Norfolk.

So I changed that summer in ways perhaps too subtle for recording. And all that I learned was absorbed into my flesh. Now I can no more isolate that learning than I can my skin. And all this writer's talk must serve as apology for my failure to absorb the one event of that summer which can be isolated. Ironic, I might say; one event of epic significance justified the setting of Norfolk that summer, and because I never learned it—this failure is how I can tell it. Yet even this much explanation is coward's stuff. For I choose the word epic with some care, and then must explain that, more than in most cases, this word describes only how the incident struck me (more accurately, how it strikes me now) and the (possibly) one or two others who observed it. George, who was the artist-in-residence that summer, comes most readily to mind. It may be simplest to begin with him.

George was maybe thirty-six, and lived not far from Norfolk the year round. Artists usually attend the summer-school once only (though musicians occasionally return), but George had grown up with the place. His father had been a gardener on the estate before it had been given to Yale, and George and his father naturally became a part of the land transaction. At the age of twenty-three George won a scholarship to the school and thereafter visited often. He lived in New York for a while, but when his father died George kept the family house, converted it to a studio and remained alone to paint as he pleased. There had been some money. His only pressure was art, and George was good enough early enough to prefer living as and where he did. He was a good artist, I eventually thought—excellent, and slowly a reputation had grown till this summer he was appointed artist-in-residence, and became a real local success.

All that I have said thus far suggests a certain relaxation in him. And I do not mislead you. He was—if an artist can be so—content. There was no material reason for him not to be. He was a more than promising artist. Recognition, however incipient, had given him confidence, had sprung his style loose from the restrictions his sense of form might have imposed on his work. His painting was disciplined, but in his pursuit of "form" he recognized no classical limitation. Oddly enough, though, a limitation existed, I have little facility in describing art, but I recall some lines from a newspaper profile I read only a few months ago. The piece began with some details about George's latest showing. Then the reviewer went on to say something like this:

> He has not permitted his obviously fertile imagination to lead him into fatal areas of the over-broadly speculative. His strokes evidence a control not common enough today in the dilettantism that so often passes for inspiration. This artist has much to tell us; more important, we will be able to understand what he has to say....

Upon first reading this I thought how George would laugh at the bullshit. My second thought was that his work could not have changed much. The fact is that even then his work appeared imaginative and daring because of the discipline each painting seemed to show in spite of itself. You had a sense that here was a craftsman's hand reining hard on a poet's imagination. The result of this tension was quite successful. And this is why I originally sneered at George's paintings. I mistrusted happy coincidence.

But I was wrong to sneer, and I liked the paintings soon enough. My instincts had not been wholly inaccurate (indeed, my intuition that summer was remarkably sensitive in all things), but I came at last to see that whatever seemed most provocative or intriguing in George's work, whatever suggested some future possibilities for the "beyond-form"—why, these intangibles, which tantalized by their very vagueness, were completed works to George. He had no sense of what lay beyond them. His disciplined technique was in no way at war with his imagination. This is why I say his painting was limited. His success lay in his never realizing the fact. He approached each subject with a pioneer's enthusiasm and left that subject, never having realized his failure to possess it. And therein lay the excellence of George's paintings: not the war, not the bullshit, but the honesty which informed everything he did.

It occurs to me that I have probably compounded the idiocy of the art critic I was just mocking. I have no better vocabulary for art. If I rightly understand what I have just written, I seem to have said that George's painting would have been bad if he had known what he was doing. And, in any event, my analysis badly distorts the simplicity of George's mind. In explaining his paintings, I may have told only of the confusion from which I have always viewed him. For I must qualify again and again. If I have suggested that he was simple, honest and limited in artistic imagi-nation, I must further say that he was witty, intelligent, socially graceful and speculative. I mistrust my record of him as I earlier mistrusted his paintings; for he was (and may still be) a good many things which I am not. I envied him much of the time and admired him the rest of it. I may, I suppose, never quite level the views. But let that much suffice for warning.

George, at thirty-six, was attractive to women. He had in addition to the glamor of art a fine body which was large, and muscled, and disciplined enough to be nearly graceful. He played tennis, ping-gong; he swam; he had wrestled. His face was not unlike mine. And as women then admired my face, so much more so did they find his face appealing. The twelve or so years that separated us had lined into his face a something as intriguing as the best of his paintings—a slightly sad history, perhaps, the nonexis-tent tragic mystery women enjoy exploring.

I do not know what the years since have told on his face; mine is no lon-ger an accurate gauge, for I do not now resemble him as he was then. But I cannot think of him without some feeling of identity. We were frequent-ly taken for brothers and in self-defense we took to letting the confusion stand. Some of my ambivalence toward George no doubt has classically psychological origins. At any rate the resemblance was a fact coloring and qualifying our relationship from the very first....

"Hi," said Karen, "Come meet George. You look just like him."

I was on leave from the Army. I had been traveling all day on three buses and a train to visit her. The last eight miles I had hitch-hiked be-cause she had got the schedule mixed up. It was late at night and I had just finally found her. Her greeting did not please me.

"I just got here." I said. "I came to see you".

She looked wonderful. She was wearing a paint-splattered work shirt and tight white shorts. Her legs, always fine, were as tanned as her face and arms. She was standing, hands on hips, legs wide apart, her head cocked slightly to the side, grinning at me. It was a pose I had never been able to resist, and I had missed her very much. In the dim light her hair was glossy, a trifle longer than usual though still cut short, pixie-like. It was jet black and I loved it. She kissed me warmly. It was not easy to remain annoyed, and I gave it up.

"Where's your uniform?" she said. "I promised everybody you'd wear your uniform. Is it in the duffel bag? It'll get wrinkled. Did you bring a Frisbee, like I asked?"

She continued chattering rapidly, lightly, about the school, about her plans for my visit, about her having missed me. And I listened and watched her as I always did with wonder and delight. And all this time we were standing about ten yards from the building called "the barn", which actually may have been a farm building at one time (though hardly a barn), and which now contains several practice rooms for musicians and a very large loft for the artists. We were just opposite the two front entrances to the two large ground floor rooms, one of which houses art exhibitions, and the other, a ping-pong table. The exhibition hall door was closed. But through the other I could see a ping-pong game in progress, and several people sitting along the sides.

Karen pulled my arm toward the open door. "Come on," she said, "meet George, and we can play a game."

There was nothing unusual in this. Both of us were good players and ping-pong was a favorite pastime. Often at Douglass when I used to visit her we would play a game or two almost at once. It was a way we had, I suppose, of re-acquaintance. Often we would do the talk of weeks apart, the conventional chatting most lovers sit down for, while volleying. We would smile and laugh and be relieved that there was sameness. And all the while our nervousness was channeled into backhands and slams, our tension released in serves and cuts and high-arcing returns. This was frequently our way and there was nothing unusual in Karen's suggestion.

But this night, fatigued and not really so eager to meet George, I wanted to go have a relaxing few beers instead—and told her so. She seemed a little puzzled that I would pass up an opportunity to see George, but agreed quickly. And we walked the winding path to the street and then down to Casey's, the only bar in town. I had a lot to tell her and we talked happily, as lovers do, all the way. I cannot recall what we said, or what I wanted to say, or if, in fact, I said any of the things I meant to. But the walk itself is as clear to me now as it was then: a warm, summer not-entirely-dark night, the rough path, the occasional streetlight, the warmth of Karen, the certainty of love. I have a few recollections of such clarity, and this is the best of them.

Just as the "barn" is divided into two rooms, each with its own entrance, so too is Casey's. The comparison ends with this fact and is no doubt whimsical anyway; for Casey's divides into a barroom and a restaurant room with booths and tables. While artists are quite likely to be found in either the ping-pong room or the exhibit room of the "barn", no student ever enters the barroom at Casey's. That room is reserved for the townsfolk, the adults, who do not like students, and who greet presumptive trespassing with looks of savage hostility. The restaurant room is large and reasonably dark.

There were a few people in the room and Karen nodded to them. But it was, on the whole, a quiet night. We sat in one of the booths and drank our beer alone. And with the tact of a Desdemona Karen kept talking of George and how much I resembled him, what a fine artist he was, how he could beat me at ping-pong. I managed one neat riposte, for which I blame the beer and the long day. I explained: "I don't resemble him. If there really is a resemblance, he resembles me."

"But he's older than you." She laughed. And, wit to the end, I clarified: "I have known me longer than him, not even having met him, and you too, so there!"

Karen thought it was funny, so I subsided, making some show at having meant it to be funny (as, indeed, I must have). And at that point in came George.

I was not really prepared to like him, and I rallied a few instant prejudices. His pants, for example, were paint-stained (though most artists at Norfolk wear their craft much more conspicuously). He wore a faded blue work shirt which was clean and pressed. I had him then as pretentious and/or hypocritical. Nor did I especially like the way he smiled at Karen. The face—well, the fact was: it was clear enough that a few unfair years had made his face more interesting; but Karen had been right. I did resemble, or he did, or somebody....

And then he spoke to me.

"You're Dick." He said. "God. She's right. I do look like you."

I was willing to be gracious. He had put it right, at least. I rose to shake his hand, and looked into his face. He was smiling at me and so were his eyes. In fact, while he was muttering the "told me so much about you" convention, he was actually looking at me. And I thought, what the hell, George, I'm glad to meet you. And then I said it.

George kept smiling. "How tired are you?" he said.

"Pretty tired. It was a long ride." I looked at Karen.

"Can you stop at my place for a beer? There's a party...I know it's your first night together, but it's a good chance to meet some people I think you'll like."

"Artists?"

"Oh yes, and musicians...."

"Musicians and singers," said Karen. It was an instrumentalist's joke. Herself a violist, Karen thought singers had an easy time of it. As an undergraduate, I had felt the same way about Math majors.

"Maybe a composite or two." said George. He winked at Karen.

"He means there are a couple of artists who play very good guitar." she said.

"One of them, Ross, plays "Cocaine" like Van Ronk." George said.

It was a magic name for me, and I suppose he had been primed for it. But, somehow, the way he said it made me feel not so very tired. I looked at Karen.

"Come on." she said. "I don't think it will spoil our night." The way she said it and the way she looked at me nearly convinced me that nothing would spoil our night.

Karen—like all girls, I guess—had a habit of making wanton bargains by suggestion, which, often enough, were never kept. She was, I knew, sincere at that moment in wanting me. But I knew also that a couple of hours could quite likely provide circumstances to make that wanting not so wanted. As I write this I wonder why men ever go to parties under such conditions. I knew then that lovers' promises are the most fragile of all; for they are the only promises which, when broken, afford not even a debating point. I had endured these trivial frustrations—more of spirit, I suspect, than of glands—from others and from Karen. So, the fact is I really do not know why we went. But, of course, we did go.

George's house was across the street from Casey's. We went, the three of us, across and up the small grass slope to the front door. For some reason that was never explained to me there is no sidewalk or driveway there, just a slightly rutted path through the grass. The night was already moist enough to wet my tennis shoes as we walked. And as we walked Karen held my arm tight—so tight—as if, I thought, she had only just realized I was there and feared my leaving again.

These were the sensations of that short walk—the wetness of the grass and the pressure of Karen on my arm. I specify them because they enclosed my last clear thoughts of that evening, the last thoughts, I should say, which took in the whole of my surroundings. For inside George's house was the chaos of many strange people and loud noises.

There were probably forty or so people in the living room, dining room, kitchen of the ground floor. They were artists mostly, though here and there an unhappy face suggested a musician. They were moving about, talking and laughing loudly—party decorum. Little knots of three or four would spin and stretch and become twelve, only to break down into more stable units. They came and went, said their joke to George and Karen, or shook hands with me and inquired loudly what I did, and would be pulled away by—I don't know—perhaps...centrifugal force. Or so it may have seemed to me. For I had spent most of my summer nights alone in the one-room apartment the Army paid for, and the entire three rooms must have been in constant motion to me: a grand wheeling microcosm to suggest—oh, large and abstract matters. (I sometimes think that way—in outward moving ripples.) And George kept us moving too, a smile, a wink, a word to keep us from encirclement. He guided us through the living room, through the dining room to the kitchen where he handed us drinks. I drank from my glass recklessly and he poured me another. It was Scotch. Then there was a rush of people into the kitchen for fresh drinks for themselves and their various partners holding the line at the many remote outpost chairs and couches. Introductions went around again. Somehow in the introducing I lost contact with the people I knew. Karen had left for the bathroom and George was at the other end of the kitchen pouring drinks. I finished my second glass too quickly and someone handed me another which I began drinking. It was bourbon. A mass offensive pulled me away into the dining room where I was suddenly being asked about painters I had never heard of.

"Excuse me," said a girl on my right, "I've got to see Bob."

She turned quickly and brushed past me. She was wearing a tight yellow sweater and I had to step back to avoid her large and not (apparently) self-conscious breasts. The sudden motion made me almost giddy. Then I was quite giddy. I leaned back against the wall, trying to stabilize the room. I slowed it by pressing both hands against my head. Then I anchored my vision to the girl in the yellow sweater. But the line rotted and fell away. As I watched her rotating her way to "Bob" I caught a glimpse of another girl staring at me, a much prettier girl. I looked at her. She had honey-colored hair. And she continued staring. I looked down at myself and realized the ungracefulness of my pose. Not all of the booze had gone to my head. Rejecting the impulse to cover myself, I turned slowly in what I hoped would be a daring and graceful pivot, and executed it not badly—except that my face collided with the top row of a bookshelf. My glass, of course, fell to the floor. I waited a moment, hoping no one had seen. My head was still fuzzy, but the blow had temporarily stopped the motion again. I knelt down to pick up the glass which was, to my surprise, unbroken. And my eyes (which insist on such things) noticed a section of several books by Josef Conrad close beside a volume of Jacobean drama. I straightened, at no small cost, and sailed purposefully toward the kitchen. I kept on course despite the eddies of humanity which moved about my wake (that's an image from "Karain", by Conrad, and it's my mind that insists on such things). I did not stop in the kitchen, but kept on out the back door. The noise and confusion receded and I gulped air and looked at the sky—somewhat overcast, I guess, for it was dark; but a few stars here and there, hundreds of light-years apart. I was leaning on the porch railing wondering why people go to parties, when behind me I heard George's voice: "Look you, the stars shine still." he quoted.

"Jesus!" I said.

It was a line from The Duchess of Malfi by John Webster. The Duchess was (and is) my favorite play, and the line quoted has fathomed centuries. At the surface it glistens clearly with the constancy of elemental things. Woven in it is the hope of an everlasting unchanging universe. If all else is flux, the stars shine still. And at this time on this drunken evening such notions partially bound me. But in the context of the play, as I well knew, the line runs deeper, darkly refracted, dragged down by turbulent undercurrents. For the Duchess has just threatened to curse the stars. Bosola replies with this cruel truth: "look you, the stars shine still." The indifference, the terrible unholy cosmic indifference of a universe that does not center on man. And in that diabolically ambiguous line, it had always seemed to me, lay the price men pay for the courage to peer through our mist and study the night.

What right had I to wrap my trivial visit to a trivial party in the grand rhetoric of a long-dead tragedian? Hypocrite to the last, I can only plead my youth and what English literature had made of my reflexes. I have heard Shakespeare quoted in Men's rooms. Why could not that boy I was appropriate some words by John Webster? For George had struck my channel accurately. The line had been on my lips as I stared at the stars while my head went round and round. And I was frightened to hear it said aloud by someone too much like me for comfort or sane belief. I didn't move a muscle.

George said, "It's nothing. Karen told me you love it. But I've always liked it too. Come on back into the mad scene. We've persuaded Ross to play for us. He's the blues guitarist we mentioned."

I straightened again. The night air had brought some clarity, but I felt very tired. I abandoned the rail and walked into the kitchen where I met Karen. The clarity I felt was not objective in any real way; rather, my mind was clear to associate and follow my association to fanciful extremes: George had said, "Come on back into the mad scene." And he had meant the party. But if he had read the play, he had also meant the scene of the Duchess's murder—the scene which includes the line I had just followed into long and devout nothingness. For to bring the Duchess to mortifi-cation, her mad brother, Ferdinand, causes madmen to be brought and placed around her. And it is in this condition that Bosola enters, twice disguised, to humble her, to say that line, to bring her to grace, to crush her spirit, to steel her courage, to humiliate, to destroy, to pity, to kill her in all the grand ambiguity that attends the affairs of men under imper-sonal stars. And seconds after her death her brother, Ferdinand, enters to accuse his hired assassin of villainy. For Ferdinand had loved her while he tortured her.

And as I looked at Karen I had a second's fantasy that she was the Duchess, that no one really knows anyone, that there was death and change around us. In short, my musing was as morbid as the finest com-edy permits.

She stood laughing at me. "You're drunk, baby." She said. "George told me about it and, honey, you are not the Duchess of Malfi."

It was a line of no less greatness in itself. She had often used it to inter-rupt some tedious existential lecture. It had always worked before, and it worked now. I drank some more Scotch. Then we went into the living room and sat on the couch George had saved for us. Nearly two-thirds of the people had left. Ross had begun to play and those who remained listened in silence.

Ross began with some conventional slow blues picking. His thumb base line was strong and steady. Reassured by the rhythm, my body began to relax. I leaned my head back to conjure the abstract visions that accompany good blues playing. I shut my eyes and listened, and my ragged nerves began to float within the soothing fluid of his melody line. Ross's hands relaxed as he warmed to his own playing. Light and sweet and delicate and so sad, he began to play and sing "Young Woman Blues".

> *I'm a young woman*
> *An' ain't done runnin' roun'*
> *I'm a young woman*
> *An' ain't done runnin' roun'....*

He played it long and well.

He paused and said something. And then he played another, and another. The music was good. Karen moved beside me and cuddled, her lips brushing lightly against my throat. The room relaxed with Ross and he played "Cocaine", played it as promised—fully as well as Van Ronk. The song eased my brain as it always does, and choked my throat a little. Ross rubbed his throat raw against that sad lyrical guitar melody, and sang as if he understood:

> *Every time me an' my baby go uptown*
> *Police come an' they knock me down*
> *Cocaine—run all roun' my brain*
> *Hey baby come here quick*
> *This ol' cocaine 'bout to make me sick*
> *Cocaine—run all roun' my brain....*
> *You take Mary I'll take Sue*
> *Ain't no difference twixt the two*
> *Cocaine—run all roun' my brain....*

"Turn em upside down," an Army friend used to say, "and they all look alike." I shook my head. Karen stirred slightly. I felt a little dizzy and I opened my eyes. Ross had begun a comic song, another Van Ronk number:

> *Mama bought a chicken well she thought it was a duck*
> *Put it on the table with its legs stickin' up*
> *In come Sis with a spoon and a glass*
> *An' starts dishin' up the gravy from its*
> *Yas Yas Yas....*

Everyone brightened, and when he had finished he asked George to sing one. It was a ritual thing, apparently, for the few people left picked up the cue and George said, "Ok, I'll sing the only one I know — if you'll help me, Ross."

"Ok. Give him the other guitar."

"Now we've done it enough. You know where the bass line goes?"

"I'm ready."

"All right. This is a Doc Watson song and Ross and I have swiped the arrangement note for note."

We all laughed and they began:

> *I was born about a thousand years ago*
>
> *There ain't nothin' in this world that I don't know*
>
> *I saw Peter Paul and Moses*
>
> *Playin' ring-around-the-roses*
>
> *An' I can whup the man that says it isn't so.*

George paused and glanced menacingly about the room for a non-existent challenger. He was magnificent, standing in the center of the room, the guitar slung round his shoulders, held rock&roll style.

> *I'm an educated man*
>
> *To get more sense within my head I plan....*

(Here Ross supplied the bass run).

> *Well I've been on earth so long*
>
> *And I used to sing a little song*
>
> *While all those old timers took their stand.*

George held up his hand for silence and Ross stopped playing. George pushed his guitar around behind him and assumed a lecture position. He had apparently done this a hundred times before and the fans were all smiling eagerly following the script, awaiting their cues.

"See how it goes?" said George. "I sing the chorus and Ross does the 'dum dum dum dum dum dum.' Now I want to say that what I really dig about this song is the chorus. I mean, can you see this guy who's been around a thousand years and is educated but is still looking for sense — can you see him just standing around singing a little song while all the great men of history took their stand? I mean, just watching and singing. There was an artist, right? Come on, it's an easy chorus. Sing along. Try it: I'm an educated man...."

Most of the people joined in cautiously and the song continued. Ritual or not, as much as I detest sing-alongs, the performance was infectious. I opened my mouth...but Karen was kissing me. And then while the people sang she grew more insistent.

"Come on," she whispered, "let's go upstairs."

By now I could barely move, but I muttered something about not leaving the party so obviously.

"It's all right. No one will notice. So what if they do?"

"George...?"

"It's all right. I already asked him. We can stay tonight."

She got up quickly and started toward the stairs. I followed more slowly. The song had ended by the time I reached the second step. By the fourth, Ross had begun to play a melody I had never heard before. I tried hard to listen, but the effort was costing me balance. I sat down suddenly on the step and in the ensuing confusion lost the first verse. That is, when I finally realized that Ross was singing, it was the chorus:

> *Green green rocky road*
>
> *Promenade in green*
>
> *Tell me who you love*
>
> *Tell me who you love*
>
> *Green green rocky road*
>
> *Promenade in green.*

"God!" I thought. "Oh God that's beautiful."

And then Karen was beside me there on the step, kissing me and whispering to me, and all I could hear was:

> *Green green rocky road. . .*
>
> *Tell me who you love. . . .*

And her hands were on me and she was sitting beside on the same step, but her weight was against me...kissing...and her hands....

> *Tell me who you love*
>
> *Tell me who you love. . .*

I could not move. She unbuttoned my shirt, moved her hands over my chest and belly. From far away they seemed to come. My skin was layered, thick. Her hands, warm musician hands, were nowhere near me—not me—but the verse continued to elude me...only the chorus:

> *Promenade in green*
>
> *Tell me who....*

I heard the sound of the zipper, not as a sound—not like the sound of music, only as a mechanical fact, the vibration's rasp on my ear drum. And then the burning, the hot intense nerve reaction as she cut through the thousand layers and touched me. She moved her hands, not rapid, frantic, but with gentleness, deliberation—musician's hands. Inside me began the screaming, drowning out the verse again...drowning. I looked at her. I could barely see her face in the dim light of the stairway. She held me. Finally I could hear her words: "I want you...I want you...now... now...I want you now...."

She let me go and stood up. I grabbed at the railing and looked after her. She stood one step above me. But after the last few seconds she seemed so far away—light-years, I thought for a sophomoric moment. I followed her slowly to the room she had arranged for us, and stood stupidly inside.

She helped me to the bed and helped me undress. I seemed almost paralyzed. It was the booze, I suppose, but my head was not spinning. Rather, I felt numbed in my head as well as my body. But she touched me again and I was not numbed; I burned and ached. She turned on the light by the bed. I lay back, tired.

"I won't be very good." I said. She was undressing.

"It's Ok." she said. "It doesn't matter. I want you."

"I can't even move, I'm so drunk."

"I'll manage." she said.

She finished undressing. She came toward the bed. My eyes were closed.

"Green green" I murmured without sound, "rocky road...promenade in green...tell me...."

"Look at me." Karen said.

I opened my eyes. She stood beside the bed, naked, and as beautiful as she had ever seemed to me—all shades and patterns in the slanted light, all hollows and surface textures—yet remote as the night sky.

"Look at me." she repeated. "Look at me."

Then she climbed on to the bed. "I want you...I want you...I want you...."

Tell me who...

Green green....

Karen made love to me. And that is how I spent my first evening in Norfolk....

JD

I had first met Karen three years before at Douglass College, which is the female part of Rutgers in New Brunswick, New Jersey. I had graduated from a small college in Pennsylvania the preceding June and, because there was nothing I wanted more to do, I had taken a job as a TV repairman's helper in Levittown, New Jersey. There I lived with my parents and repaired TV's and read and wrote a little.

A friend I had known at my college had transferred to Rutgers and invited me to visit him. His name was JD. He was an artist and I liked him. Together with two other friends who wrote poetry we had formed a kind of club through the summer. It was the usual sort of thing. We visited New York often together and we wrote witty and insulting letters back and forth. A specialty of ours was the writing of arcane verse filled with clues and suggestions for, as we said it, "the grad students".

Certain of fame as we all were, the necessity for obscuring our lives to future biography was our particular pride and pleasure. Sometimes we patterned ourselves on the Hunt-Keats-Lamb crowd, sometimes on the Georgians. It depended on the mood of the time, as did the roles we assumed within our group. I preferred Keats, I suppose, though I was usually the leader. So the letters went the quadrangle—strange mixtures of daily doings and scraps of un-footnoted verse. And that had been our summer into September.

But one sold out to Temple grad school and another joined the Army. By October I had all but lost contact even with JD. So I accepted his invitation and visited him at Rutgers. I went on a Friday night and stayed through the week-end.

That Friday night we spent drinking at the favorite student bar. It is named Mosco's, though inevitably pronounced Moscow's. Very good Italian food and, more important, large scoops of draft-beer are served there.

It is only four blocks from the Douglass campus and, despite a perfunctory check of I.D. cards, it is not difficult for under-age girls to be served at Mosco's. It is usually very crowded and was so this night. We were drinking in the back room, which is where the students drink. (I do not think I need be embarrassed to point out that Mosco's, too, divides into "town" and "student" sections, each with its own entrance. Most college town bars have the same arrangement.) The back room is large enough for several tables of different sizes, much too close to each other for comfortable movement among them.

We had taken a small table at the side, strategically near the Dutch-door whose upper half functions as a serving and ordering window. The room was noisy but, seated to the side, we were at least spared the confusion which characterized most of the room. We drank our beer and observed the collisions around us. For us it was very much a literary evening and we cherished our relative isolation—symbolic, as we said.

We began, of course, with talk of our two lost friends. While near us chairs crashed and glasses spilled, JD and I maintained a lofty nostalgia. Our toasting was witty and arduous. Our missing comrades had, after all, much to be wished good fortune and health for—particularly Pete, the one in the Army. But eventually, having covered all of Pete's possible promotions, and having exhausted the permutations of Jacobean puns on potato-peeling, we found ourselves left with ourselves.

JD solved the dilemma by proposing that we drink to the next drink, and I, touched by the infinite implications of his ingenuity, assented. We had got to our feet (after some difficulty) and were holding our glasses aloft when we heard a terrible crash beside us. A loosely associated group, two men and four girls, had entered the room. They had attempted to squeeze through the center toward our table, and the first four had managed the journey without incident. But the fifth, a clean-cut looking type, had tripped over someone's foot and had fallen heavily against the large table nearest us. Every drink on the table had spilled. Beer was pouring in attractively random design across the table, along it, into laps and shoes, and on the floor. People at the table were leaping up and away from the flood, brushing at their clothes and shaking their wrists and forearms dry. Two waiters were rushing in with mops, while people at other tables rose expectantly for the possible fight. The clean-cut type helped with the mopping, apologizing to everyone; but his five companions continued to our table where they greeted JD, laughing with us at the chaos. They were friends of his, and among them was a very pretty girl—who was, of course, Karen.

You may by now have the impression that I was in those days often drunk, or, at least, often drunk with Karen. But this is not the case, and I hasten to correct the impression as I hastened that night to sober myself. The fact is, I drink rarely and almost never to excess, and I was very much attracted to her. I have since wondered why—what, specifically, it was about her that impressed me. Through chance, it seemed, she was unattached that night, and she appeared interested in me almost from the first. No doubt this helped; for I should say that, while I had had my share of girls, I had not yet learned that I was personally attractive. I felt unsure and happily astonished when girls liked me. So her interest in me was partly the cause—but a minor part, I think. She was very pretty—or perhaps "cute" would be more appropriate; for her attractiveness was conventiona1. And this fact makes my reaction doubly puzzling; for my taste in those days was for the more unusual, the beatnik type.

Karen's hair was black and beautiful—her best single feature, I think—but cut short. She was not more than five feet tall, with a slim, rather boyish figure. And her face was—well, cute. She looked, in short, like most Douglass girls—not, certainly, my usual type. But something made me hurry to the Men's room and splash cold water on my face. And something made me sip nervously from one beer the rest of the evening. For now, let us call it an attraction.

Clean-cut's victims had left the room to repair their damaged suits and psyches, and our group took over the large table. There was some joking about it as "spoils of war", and a metaphor from JD about beer and blood. Our group seemed determined to restore the previous condition, and beer began to appear again in glasses and in puddle-form here and there on the table. At the far end, Clean-cut was recharging his ego by retelling the adventure, repeating the jokes, a little more loudly each time. He had been lucky to escape without a fight and he knew it. Half way down from him sat a rather drunken JD who added, in a malicious style, a line or two to each retelling. These were not his most sensitive friends and JD was anxious that I should know he knew it. Clean-cut seemed to ignore him and the others were tactfully neutral. Karen sat beside me and we conversed quietly apart.

I have no real recollection of what we talked about at first. The usual openers, I suppose. I know that when she asked me what I did for a living I felt a bitterness I had not known before, and nearly ruined the scene by being very defensive about TV repair. She did not, as I recall it, press me on the subject, but talked about her music, showed me the callouses on her fingers, and joked about how violists cannot have long fingernails. She didn't seem to mind. And she talked about my hands—which are small for a man, with long tapering fingers. They are "artistic" hands, no doubt delicate, and I have hated them since I can remember.

"Do you play anything?" she asked.

"Only ping-pong."

She laughed. "That's a myth anyway. Musicians have stubby fingers. Ping-pong? really? Are you good?"

"I'm a champion."

"Oh I love to play. I'm not bad...for a girl."

"Let's have a game sometime, then."

"Ok." She smiled as if the idea really pleased her.

We were, of course, playing a different game then, and I did all I could to mitigate the TV repairman image. I came on shamelessly:

Faulkner is all right so long as you don't take him seriously....

La Dolce Vita is about modern man's search for meaning—tautological, I suppose; but then clichés are often only inevitably restated truths....

Wild Strawberries...oh, you like *Wild Strawberries*? *The Seventh Seal* is my film...I think people reveal themselves in that choice...don't you agree?... yes....

No, I can't read O'Neil...I can't read anything post-Seventeenth century...not drama, anyway—except maybe Beckett....

Keats...above all, Keats...well he's actually Seventeenth century in sensibility...only Shakespeare or Webster....

JD had caught the drift by now and was amused enough to help in a kind of drunken, not very useful way. "Tell her about our composite poems." he said. (Believe it or not, he pronounced it composhit.) Karen's eyes laughed a little, but her face never broke.

I hurriedly told her of the composite sonnets the four of us had written in a cafe at New Hope once when we were feeling particularly European; how each one of us in turn added a line until we had three quatrains; then how we broke the couplet into two and a half feet each—"no small feat, either", I am afraid I added. To my surprise, things at the end of the table had calmed a bit, and we were a conversational group again. Clean-cut even commented, "Oh, Shakespearean sonnet."

I nodded forgiveness toward him while the other guy explained the difference to the three girls. At least I assume that is what he was doing. I heard the word Petrarchan just before Karen said, "Can you do one now?"

"Well," I said, "there are only two of us...."

JD came in on cue: "I'm drunk. Do one of your impromptu sonnets. That ought to Impresh the hell out of everyone."

I glared; he chuckled. Like most of us he was at least half actor, and his drunk "role" he had derived from bad movies.

"How do you do it?" said Karen.

"You tell me the form and the topic, then give me ten minutes, and I write it."

I could do it, all right. It was a ritual performance. It had begun when Pete, having read of the Keats-Hunt "Grasshopper and the Cricket" contest, challenged me to try it. We had been, as I have suggested, very much caught up in the idea of being a literary movement. We were all extremely facile, but rhymes and image-clusters came easiest to me—and this is the measure of such writing. I had won the first and I won thereafter. The poems were not usually very good, but occasionally I would strike fire. Most

I tore up; but I had sweated a few into fair poems. In the kind of group we were it was my most admired work.

So I could do it. But secretly I had begun wondering if this fatal facility was not destroying me as a poet. And in the few weeks preceding this visit I had been writing in very rough hard sounds and the loosest of metres. To be honest, it had become more than a wondering or even a doubt. I had recently felt more than once that my entire manuscript collection showed nothing more than promise; that I had to break into a new form; that if I was ever to be more than a literate young man with a file of excellent and polished exercises, I had to write a real poem—and write it soon. My preparation for this "real" poem had been, I was beginning to think, fatally methodical. I had torn each potential poem out of my head before the poem had had a chance to work itself out, and then I had jammed it into a form it had not naturally selected. Having read somewhere of a similar crisis in Browning's career, I adopted his tactics, revising out every connective, declaring war on articles and clause adjectives. I had worked hard, but so far I had produced nothing but crabbed inversions of my usual verse. And now I was at a table with a group of people, most of whom probably would not know the difference, hoping very much to be able to recall that old smooth facility—this to impress a girl who, I feared, might know the difference.

One of the girls across the table said, "How about an epic?"

"In ten minutes?" I laughed. Then, because I saw she was not just trying to be funny, I made an effort at extricating her—with, I will admit, the additional motive of covering my doubt in style: "No epics in the Twentieth century." I said.

JD snorted, spilling his beer.

"Why?" said Karen. "Is it the competition with TV?"

She was on my side, unless she had referred to my week-day profession.

"A matter of shenshibillty." said JD. "No more dragons or Holy wars or God or that crap."

The girl who had suggested epic laughed to show that she was modern and agnostic and all that.

"What do you think?" Karen asked me.

I thought for a second. Then I said, "Why don't I write what I think?"

"Damn right!" said JD. "Alwaysh write what you think."

It was a gamble, though perhaps on the cheating side. For the subject had caused me a good deal of thought before now. There just might be a poem in my head.

"Yesh," said JD, "alwaysh write what you think. When you drink, you shtink, but you write what you think..." He went on like that for a minute, while I tried to sort out my head. Karen put her hand on his arm. He stopped.

"Yes," he said, "a sonnet, I think, would be appropriate."

I took out the notebook which I had brought to show my latest efforts to JD, and I poised my pen. A general drink ordering distracted my audience for a few seconds. Then the other guy began telling a story about an astrologer he had once known. The three girls expressed interest, one to the point of holding up her palm for a reading. The other guy explained the difference. JD stared at his watch, Karen watched me. Clean-cut interrupted the story: "Do you really swallow that stuff? Stars! for Chrissakes!"

"No," said the other guy, "but how can you be sure? Look... even this glass of beer reacts the way tides do."

"Whadda you mean?"

"I mean the moon. All liquids get pulled by the moon. It can be measured. Even a glass of beer...well, a glass of water, anyway. It can be measured. They've done it. When you think of your body and how it's mostly liquid...."

My audience was being entertained. The voices receded, blended with the general noise of the room. I had been writing for some time.

The first stanza came quickly. I had decided to begin by brutalizing epic themes. And this was the result:

> *Achilles' bladder probably required*
>
> *A draining, like Napoleon's and my own;*
>
> *The hero stuff, flesh even then retired:*
>
> *He tried, he died, endures through verse alone.*

I still had no idea what my position would be, but I was confident now. The old empty, wittily toned facility was there for the tapping, I could still do it. The third line was even, perhaps, good.

I now began the second stanza. And as I began thinking it, suddenly the sestet began breaking through. I scribbled just a word or two for the second stanza, and leaped to the end. I was by now—like no previous impromptu writing time—genuinely excited by the words I used, by the discovery of what I thought, what I was. I finished the sestet and returned to the second stanza. I wrote its last two lines, then the first and second. Quickly, not really reading the whole, not really daring to do so, I scanned the poem, revised three words. I looked up. I had not noticed it, but conversation had stopped. Everyone was watching me.

"Fourteen and a half minutes." said JD, shaking his head.

"Shlipping, old man. Let's hear it."

"I'd like a cigarette." I said.

Karen offered me one of hers. "Please read it," she said.

I had no matches. I slapped at all my pockets. Karen struck a match for me. I leaned forward and lit the cigarette. I took an authorial puff, and messed it up by coughing. Then, holding the notebook in one trembling hand, I read:

> *Achilles' bladder probably required*
> *A draining, like Napoleon's and my own;*
> *The hero stuff, flesh even then retired:*
> *He tried, he died, endures through verse alone.*
>
> *And if he fought a fight, his carcass fed*
> *A similar stuff as Hector's. And to know it,*
> *Makes my event heroic. Our time dead*
> *For Epic? No the lack is — epic poet.*
>
> *For I could tell a tale of greater glories.*
> *Of daily measurings against an Age*
> *(To wash your epics thin as bed-time stories),*
> *A time of Electricity and Rage,*
>
> *Of men swinging beneath impersonal stars —*
> *Of passion-less dragons called subway cars.*

I finished reading. My audience was impressed. So was I. To be sure, there were dead spots—Napoleon, for example, and the absurd "fought a fight...fed". The first eight lines were, as a whole, clumsy doggerel, very much impromptu (though I could live several weeks on the phrase, "makes my event heroic". Event! God, what a choice for death!). But the sestet—there was the triumph. The wonderful live sestet! I had reservations. I was not sure if "wash thin" worked the way I wanted it to. But, so what? Revision. Much time for that. The practice had worked, somehow. The couplet was new to me, new to my work and style. It rang harsh and vibrant, moving as the thought did—from smooth to hard. It was not metre and rhyme; it was rhythm and sound—a real poem. The germ of a real poem.

I was so excited, I forgot to ask to drive Karen back to her dormitory. When the exodus began it was too late.

Later, back in JD's apartment, I thought about Karen. "I think it's very good." she had said. And I had let her go. I lay back on the couch and marvelled, not for the first time, at my limitless incompetence. Her eyes were brown and they looked straight at you. Brown eyes always seem a little sadder—a little wiser, too. Why is that? "I think it's very good." she had said. But why don't we write what we think?

I got up and went into JD's room. "Tell me about Karen." I asked. He was very sleepy. He had spent his last energy in getting me some extra blankets, and he could barely talk:

"Huh? Oh...she's Ok...pretty great ass...I wouldn't mind...." His voice fell off. Then it was loud again for one last sleep-preceding statement:

"That was a fucking good poem. You sonofabitch. I should carry my sketchbook around."

I returned to my couch. I thought of Karen for a long while. Then, like a child with a Christmas present, I got out my poem and reread it. For the first time I read not the sounds and constructions, but the how of it—the whole poem. I put it away and lay back still thinking of it. I thought then that I knew what had attracted me to Karen....

Authorial Note

With acute embarrassment, I find as I reread my draft that, whereas I evidently intended specifically to explain this last cryptic sentence, in point of fact, I have not done so till much later in the narrative. The reader will, I should hope, surmise before too long that the attraction I speak of has to do with an existential response I felt immediately in Karen. Surely there has been and will be enough discussion of my obsession with The Duchess to make the point clear. All that grand rhetoric at George's party, and the "impersonal stars" crap. But the next immediate digression is to ping-pong. Since the "poet" business has been pushed to the limit just now, maybe I should break in here with some personal introduction of myself. What do you think? The ping-pong stuff gets self-conscious so maybe that'll do it. And there is coming fairly soon a more formal personal interruption. But maybe, since I've been kind of ironic about myself here anyway, maybe I should lay it on a bit. The thing is —what diction? I like the reader to know I'm conscious of my pose, and he's already seen me relax a lot. Perhaps JD's diction makes this a good place for transition.

Douglass Student Center

JD and I both slept late the next morning. It was sunlight that roused me finally. It had moved gently and unobtrusively around his apartment to stream finally in through the windows above my couch. I had slept well, and I greeted the sun with affection; it seemed a good omen.

I awoke JD, who affected the foul mood of a hang-over and refused to get up for still another hour. I spent the time preparing and drinking some instant coffee I found in his kitchen. I made some for him, too, and delivered it. Then I read a magazine and waited for some response.

Finally he stumbled out of his room, muttering a vague "thanks" for the coffee. "Let's go get some breakfast," I said. He nodded sleepily and yawned. He sat down in an easy-chair and stared out the window for a minute. Then he stood up. "Douglas Student Center," he said, then added (with surprising humor) "Don't forget your notebook."

It was now mid-afternoon. Saturday afternoons, the student center is nearly deserted; we ate alone and in silence. JD either stared murderously at his coffee cup or obscenely at the pelvis of each of the few girls that passed. There were maybe five or six of them. His mood amused me, as his moods usually did. Perhaps because he was our only painter, he was the cynic of our brotherhood. But I was happy. It was an unusual Autumn day—not really crisp enough for football, different from Spring, however—a day of much warmth. The windows near our table were open, and even indoors there was a sense of trees and grass—that kind of nice romantic thing. I had not forgotten my note book; it lay comfortably between my foot and the table leg. Nor had I forgotten Karen.

She arrived at a fortunate moment. JD had just left to get us more coffee from the snack-bar. She came directly to the table and stood smiling at me. She looked as good as she had last night—better, perhaps, for now she had exchanged her black sweater for a red one; her black hair glistened beautifully beside it.

I leaped to my feet, "Sit down," I said. And she did.

"I thought you'd be here." she said.

"Why?"

"Because you forgot to ask me for a date."

Her head was cocked slightly to the side. Her eyes sparkled, little flecks of amusement danced lightly. I imagine I blushed.

"I know, I also forgot to take you home."

"It was ok. I understood. It was the poem, wasn't it?"

"Yes."

She glanced at the notebook on the floor. "May I read it again?"

Honesty can be infectious. "No," I said.

"Why?"

"Because it's not finished. Last night it was a stunt, but now I think it's an unfinished poem."

She nodded thoughtfully and we looked at each other for a while. Then JD was back with the coffee. "I see," he said, "the neatest ass in all of Douglass has condescended to a seat at our humble table."

She only laughed at him.

"Who's your friend?" I said to her.

"I thought he was with you."

We both sneered at JD. I have what I like to think of as a "withering sneer". The left corner of my lip lifts and wrinkles clear up to above my nostrils. A half-effort is effective; the full treatment is irresistibly comic. It was the comic one I used here, and Karen duplicated it perfectly.

JD put down the coffee. "All right," he said, "let her have it. I'll go persuade some existential baby to make the nude scene."

We watched him go. "Will he?" said Karen.

"I don't know. You know him better here than I do. He says it's a square place."

"He does all right, I guess. New Brunswick is funny...it's square and not square...I've heard...I think he does all right. I went out with him once. He's direct—I'll say that."

"His motto..." I paused, "it's...go right for the box. He claims the shock is worth a few points."

She laughed. "That's it, all right. That's what he does. It's a little crude to score. I think he can paint, though."

"Yes, I think so too."

"And you can write." She stood up. "Can you play ping-pong? I don't really want this coffee."

The ping-pong table was downstairs from the cafeteria. We played for nearly an hour. She was very good—for a girl. I enjoyed the games. I enjoyed watching her, listening to her. Some people you can talk to across a ping-pong table. I don't know why it is. You don't have to shout or repeat yourself; they hear you. With such persons the normal rules are suspended. The inane jokes that make up most table tennis conversation do not seem needed. When the ball tips the net and falls over for a point, one feels no need to say brightly, "save those for the game." With such people, one feels free to say "good shot", and mean it. The well-intentioned "good try" does not rankle.

There is something primeval about table tennis, as about all sport. Jungian symbolism may or may not provide an accurate explanation. I do not know if the spheres of most sports have some "egg" ancestor. I do know that the explanation is inadequate for my feelings about sport. Players undoubtedly engage in a ritual ceremony of sorts, and—in a large sense—"fertility" may be a label for the ceremony; but the contest has shadows of barbarity that darken beyond any easy word like "fertility". Sex is inherent, of course, as it is in all violence—or so people have convinced me (and since the vocabulary belongs to those people the concept cannot be refuted). I think, though, that sex or violence are not very useful terms either.

There are body-contact sports which particularly invite Freudian analysis. And there are body-contact sports, such as basketball and baseball, which pose as non-contact sports. I do not hunt or fish; so I know nothing of blood-sports (which seem rather obvious anyway). Then there is a group of sports which are by nature competitive in an abstracted way, sports in which each contestant directs himself more toward a goal than against a man. Golfers and Track-men will disagree, for both have felt the pressure of competition. Yet my classification is generally correct. If they play their sport as well as they can, their opponent does not matter—ideally at least. (Dart-shooting is the nearest I have been to this kind of sport. And I have, of course, lost games because of competitive pressure. It is, I must insist, though, an abstracted pressure. And rich though dart-shooting may be in the most obvious atavisms, I have never had the sense that I was symbolically impaling an opponent. The action was too remote.)

Tennis comes closest to what I think informs table tennis. And in some ways tennis seems more obviously violent. There is the very strenuous exercise and the hard hitting. The serve itself represents a direct and savage attack on a real opponent. Occasionally it is. But tennis, too, has an elusive remoteness. A man could play many sets without developing a sense of real contact with his antagonist. The distance is too great. The other man seems small, often faceless.

Of the action sports, table tennis alone in my experience presents the truest non-contact ritual of violent contest between two communicating personalities. Does the rhetoric seem fulsome? Blame the "ologists" who have warped our language out of innocence. When I speak of table tennis I speak of a sport whose common name precludes serious discussion. Ping-pong. Children. The family recreation room. Only tidily-winks, perhaps, is more ludicrous. Ping-pong has come to be a game kit under the tree at Christmas, a problem of space for planning parents, something the Orientals play very well in that comic, quick- moving style they use. For most people ping-pong is: two girls holding their paddles wrong, hitting awkwardly at an elusive ball; the sound: clop...(long pause)...clop...giggle...miss.

Everyone realizes, of course, that some people play it fast and well. Indeed, there is one such, probably, in every group. But is it not a trivial excellence? Most who excel at table tennis feel some slight guilt about its triviality. Playing table tennis is rather like writing poetry. Certainly an expert deserves admiration, but is the accomplishment really very significant? A generation of anti-romantic poets supports me, but the simile is exaggerated. Poetry is, after all, culture. So—thanks to Hemingway—are some sports. But the dignity of table tennis suffers from an irony inherent in its unique status as the most stylized, sophisticated of the active, face-to-face battle-sports. The more sophisticated, the more symbolic, the more removed from the primeval—the more trivial.

Yet there it is. Two players bang away at each other with weapons whose name has not the brute honesty of "club" or "bat", or the typographical elegance of "racquet". Two players attack each other with things called paddles, in a drastically confined area which permits no large audience. These players are close enough to feel, to sense each other. The slam is a genuine assault; the return, an archetypal nose-thumbing.

Between experts the game is fast, but the ball hangs in the air often—a lovely controlled thing—and the spectator has time to witness it all: a man slams. the other cuts-under. two, perhaps three slams more, each returned by an undercut, yet each return a bit stronger. almost imperceptibly the condition has changed. the men are hitting equally now. a sharp placement. the slammer must give ground, return weakly. The former defender now slams. It is a duel. It is Newton's Third Law.

A game is won when one man scores twenty-one points (with, of course, a margin of two). Theoretically, all strokes may be returned by an expert. And it is a fact that between two excellent players there are few outright placement scores. Errors, then, account for most of the forty points scored in a good game. Even for the victor there have been perhaps nineteen mistakes. The scoring system reveals the game. Nineteen errors for the winner! nineteen mistakes! misjudgments! wounds! cuts! scars! Other sports have dramatized the poor-loser, but the ragged splinter edge of the average ping-pong table tells most accurately the origins of this game.

I have played table tennis since I was a boy. This "Knights and Squires" digression no doubt falls from a most deeply rationalized niche in my very complex head. The point of it all was, I think, to imply something about character. For I know that while playing I develop an intuitive sense of my opponent. Aggressive players are aggressive people; defensive players are not. That seems obvious enough. But there remains something in the playing that is not so easily divisible as slam and return. An extension of personality is in each stroke. I have not always been able to see it clearly. But some people I enjoy playing, and others irritate me. Winning or losing does not cover the difference. When volleying or playing with Karen, I was aware of a subtle contact.

She played, as I've said, quite well. She had a graceful but very vigorous masculine style—almost a tennis style—though she had never learned to slam. She hit the ball hard, but with a swooping, long stroke that was not a slam. Only now and then, in the most unlikely moments, she would suddenly back-hand the ball in a surprisingly unorthodox way. She would fall back—almost—and bring the paddle around and over her left shoulder, off-balance, awkward. It was a hard slam, but it rarely hit the table. For three years I tried to talk her out of it. She used it seldom, and occasionally it would hit. When it landed, it always scored, and, of course, there went my argument.

We played that Saturday until I knew her. We talked and hit the ball back and forth. There were long silences which were not strained or awkward. There were jokes, but they were not ping-pong jokes. When the ball hit her breast, I felt no need to comment with the usual embarrassed wit. She felt no need to laugh or to blush. When we stopped, I complimented her. She accepted and told me I was the best she had ever played. It was probably the truth.

She had lost the last point when one of my slams hit the net and just ticked the side of the table. She thought, laughing, that it was a good time to stop. I resisted the ping-pong joke about practising those net shots. (Though, in truth, as a boy I actually had practised hitting the ball at the top of the net. I'd set up a practice board in the attic where we had our table. It was a converted dining table, much shorter than regulation. (I've always felt the shortness helped me achieve a special control.) I used to spend hours playing alone, hitting—one bounce on the table on the other side of the net, then the rebound off the board, and back to my side. I invented whole teams of players, with elaborate schedules and complicated scoring rules. I kept all records and still have some of them. The point was, supposedly, the practice, and I awarded bonuses for shots off the top of the net. The bonuses were necessary because these shots would end the volley—no possible rebound; and, you see, I usually scored according to the number of successive strokes before the volley was broken. But I had to have a purpose—practice—or the games would have degenerated into solitary fun. So the net shot doubled the score or something like that, if you took your chances and hit close to the net. Thus, actually, I had practised net-hitting. This was my reason—though the names of the players in my mythical leagues were those of real people, football stars.)

I resisted the joke; instead, I began a story: "Once when I was in a tournament...." And then I stopped.

Karen looked at me. "Go on."

I put my paddle down on the table. "I just remembered how I came on last night."

She came over and sat down on my half of the table, her left side to the net. She composed herself for a story. "Go ahead. Tell me."

I watched her take the ball and place it on the table against the paddle so that the ball rested in the corner where the handle connects to the paddle-part. Then I sat beside her on the table.

"Well, once I was playing in the finals of a tournament, the last game. We'd tied two each. It was a best-out-of-five thing. And we'd got to deuce. I was nervous and I played patty-cake. So was he, for that matter. It was funny, I guess, because we'd both been slamming like hell, and now — two cautious guys, little weak safe shots, all slammable, and neither one with nerve enough to slam. And then I got too cautious and hit into the net. It was as stupid a thing as I've ever done. That put me one down. It was my serve and I was so seared I'd muff the serve, I set it up — high, with nothing on it at all. He was confident enough with his one point to slam it, and it hit hard near the corner...."

She ducked back, I'd been flailing my arms, demonstrating throughout, very conscious of the awkwardness of demonstrating a story while sitting side-to. She'd finally acknowledged my problem, and she smiled to show me it was a joke.

"I'm sorry." I continued, "It was a good slam — perfect, if it had been to the backhand. I had a weak backhand then. Well I just kind of swiped at it out of desperation, and it sailed out wide of the table by a couple of inches. I mean that's some idea of how hard he hit it, because I'd swung forehand and I'd tried to hit it across the table, not down the same side that is. I suppose that's what I'd meant, because it's the safe shot, and I really wasn't thinking at all — just trying to hit it...."

Karen laughed "Get on with it."

"Well, that's my style. That's how I tell stories. I go around like that. Things keep coming up that I should explain...."

She kissed me. Just like that. There we were sitting on the ping-pong table and she just kissed me. It was light and very sweet. I was startled.

"Go on," she smiled, "finish the story."

It was a remarkably stupid thing to do, but I actually could think of nothing better than to continue the story.

"So, it was wide of the table by a couple of inches...." (I was hurrying now.) "and you know how time seems to slow down sometimes and you see things very clearly?" (She nodded.) "Well, I can see that ball just as clearly. It sailed very slowly and...look...see this metal post? Well it hit the top of the post like this...." (I leaned across her to demonstrate.) "and for some reason bounced back toward the table and...." (Here I grazed the edge of the table directly where the net and the table join. I let the ball drop to the floor, where it bounced a few times and finally lay still, resting against the wastebasket.) "of course he couldn't get it. Think now, it had been traveling out; it should have been a complete miss."

I thought it was a pretty good story, and it had actually happened. But I felt now that the story was distinctly anti-climactic. How do you top a kiss? I had done my bit, and now felt rather foolish. But Karen seemed interested in the story.

"Did it count?" she asked.

A few more sentences at least before the next silence—I jumped at the chance, I could always talk.

"They had quite a conference about it. But they ruled that the metal post was part of the net, and allowed it. He was furious."

"And...?"

"He did just what I'd been afraid of. He hit his serve too hard and missed the table. He returned my next serve, but I wasn't nervous anymore and I slammed the hell out of it. I kind of figured the fates had given it to me.... I want to talk about what you did."

"We," she said, "You helped."

I laughed, I was nervous so I laughed.

"What do you want to say about it?" she said.

"I guess...I guess I just want to do it again."

So we kissed again. You must consider the insanity of it. Atop a ping-pong table in the afternoon in the Douglass Student Center we—I, anyway—kissed with all the shy sweet nervousness of a thirteen-year-old. I knew no explanation, still know none except the genuine poetic evasion, love. Yet there we sat and kissed happily, tenderly, our legs dangling like a modifier from the edge of the table.

We sat there for some time. And I do not know what, if anything, was in my head until my eye, unobtrusively following the line of her leg, noticed the ping-pong ball near the wastebasket. Simultaneously, a tune came into my head. I looked straight down at the floor.

"I hope you don't start humming." I said.

"What?"

"It's a book, Studs Lonegan, by James Farrell. Studs has one great day in his life. He beats up the neighborhood bully, and walks Lucy home. On the way they sit on a tree limb, and she hums "In the Blue Ridge Mountains of Virginia". And they dangle their feet in the air...like this...."

"Why not." I was not facing her, but her tone suggested both that she knew the answer and that it did not matter.

"It's the last good day he ever has. He lives nineteen or so more years waiting for something to happen. And it never does. He just keeps re-living that day, feeding on it, and eventually he dies."

"Oh." It was a way of saying: this is not the most flattering method of telling me this is a great day for you.

"I'm sorry. It's the way I am. I can't help making associations like that. The book impressed me. I used to think I was Studs Lonegan."

"I don't think so." She had eased off the table and was facing me. It made me sadder yet, and I began whining.

"Oh, I'm better educated and smarter, but I have the same ill-defined dreams...."

"I don't think you're Studs Lonegan. Let's go eat." She could do it. She could cut it off like that.

So we went to dinner. I laid out the bulk of my remaining cash for a lavish Italian meal. We dined in candle-lit splendor, consumed wine, and talked like lovers.

"What shall we do tonight?" I asked, as we were drinking our coffee.

"We'll go to a movie." she said. "My treat."

It flustered me; a nervous hand shot toward my pocket.

"No." she said, "It's no use. I saw how you counted your money...before, when I was coming back from the ladies room. And I'm only teasing. The movie's free. They show a movie at The Ledge every Saturday night. It's noisy, but they have some good movies."

"What's The Ledge?"

"It's the Rutgers Student Center, my poor poet friend. It's full of rude young drunks, and I shall require an escort. OK?"

"Kismet." I said. "Do we have time for more coffee?"

We did, and the waiter refilled our cups. Karen took a sip, slowly, thoughtfully.

"That's twice." she said.

"Twice?" I was busily stirring my coffee. I looked up at her. Her expression was serious. A glaze of thought moved across her eyes.

"Yes, twice. Kismet—that's fate, isn't it?"

I feared, for a terrible moment, that she was going to say something trite and girlish about our meeting. "Yes." I said.

"Well, you said you were fated to win the ping-pong game. That's twice."

"Ah—it was written."

"But last night—" she was looking at me, possibly, as other people inquire one's religion. "the poem...swinging under impersonal stars...."

She had almost remembered the line. This was more than flattering.

38

But I was not about to repeat my performance of last night. No! This was an evening for wit, not for philosophy.

"It's very simple." I said. "My successes are my own; my failures aren't. That's how I think of it. Most people do."

But I had spoken too quickly and too lightly for conviction. She simply looked puzzled.

"But that's all twisted around," she said. "Your ping-pong game wasn't a failure."

The one girl in a thousand who could follow an abstraction with logic, and I had to play games.

"A detail." I said.

She smiled, a little nervously, I thought. "You just don't want to talk about it because you don't think I'll understand."

I gulped at my coffee. First Studs Lonegan, now this; but I really had little choice. There was silence for a minute. Then I began:

"What I said..." (my tone now carried conviction) "was true enough. I think most people—and me—consider the "free will" business when it suits them. But the idea of fate has a few problems anyway. When you say "fate", do you mean psychological determinism, or a random pattern, or God? And if you mean God, is it a hostile God, or a deist God, or what? I mean, it's an easy word."

I suppose I was serious enough. She listened gravely, and seemed to be thinking about it. Then she began the coffee stirring not with my casualness, though; she merely toyed with the spoon. She stared at the coffee.

"Things don't care, do they?" she said.

"I don't think so. But if they do...you mean nature or the universe? something like that?"

She nodded.

"Well, whether they are hostile or indifferent, we're still left rather helpless. And since I've never till this week-end seen any evidence that things work out for the best—I don't really believe the universe is kind."

So I was to be the one, girlish and trite—"till this weekend", indeed! But she let it go.

"Why...?" she began. And then she smiled. "I was about to ask something really stupid and female."

"Oh," I said quickly, "it's an old problem, and not an awfully useful one. The Elizabethans...."

"Yes." she said. "JD mentioned a play...something, I think it was, about being...." She frowned it into recollection. "the stars' tennis-balls." She laughed suddenly. "Ping-pong balls!"

"We are the stars' tennis-balls, struck and bandied which way please them." I gave it my reading voice.

"That's it. But doesn't the same person say something else later?"

"Look you, the stars shine still?"

"Yes, that's it."

"He says it earlier. It's Bosola, and he says it earlier. In the context it might mean a change...." I stopped. "What did JD say I thought?"

She looked uncomfortable, caught and uncomfortable. She decided on honesty; "He said that you thought since either way the person is helpless, the playwright...."

"John Webster."

"Webster...probably didn't care about the difference."

This was, in fact, my opinion at the time—an opinion I had insisted upon with my friends at much length on several occasions. I looked closely at Karen. Her eyes were downcast. She looked at the tablecloth a while. Then she looked up shyly, perhaps flirtatiously.

"Are you mad at me?" she said.

"No."

"I did it. It's true. JD talked about it a lot...and you, too...and I knew it was your favorite play and you even planned to do it some time. I knew you'd like to talk about it. But it wasn't just female, you know. I'm interested, I'm very interested. I want to learn about...I'm being stupid. Are you mad?"

Had I ever heard a more honest speech? With commendable gallantry I brushed it aside.

"I'm only annoyed with JD for using my line." (How contagious honesty can be!) I said grandly. "The rest is too flattering.... Anyway," I added, "the tennis-ball business is in Pericles, too. And I'm damned if I know what that play's about."

Perhaps "gallantry" is too strong a word. The fact is, I didn't care at all. I felt happy that she had troubled to plan for me. An absurd giddiness rose to my head from out of a coffee cup.

We left soon after, hurrying for the movie. And as we passed through the door, she took my arm.

"It's a good line." she whispered. "But it works better when you do it."

Fond Memories

Such scattered thoughts, bits of dialogue, pieces of trivia—these are my cargo. There is ballast too, of invention, of organization; but, as such voyages go, very little. The time-travel that is recollection is not often selective. But in this recounting there has been little need for steering. A first day with anyone who becomes important to your life may remain remarkably defined for much of that life. There will be a clear record of some dialogue, much of thought, and even more of setting. As years pass and superimpose other scenes, some confusion will, of course, occur. Then, at that point, memory will become toned by the subjective matter of the intervening years.

My life often seems to me a shadow of what is actually occurring. So often do I travel in my memory, I wonder if I am not—in some more than metaphoric way—a ghost. When my depressions wear me, they are of this nature and form: that my only reason for each day's activity may be the stocking of more memory-tapes for some future travelogue. This fear has some physiological basis, for I know that the reaction time of the best coordinated athlete is no less than one-sixth of a second. That is, the fastest of us live our lives this much in the past. Sophistry, I suppose—given the relativity concepts. Yet as I age, and as I feel my muscles wither, I know that I fall further back of fact. And with this decay, so grows progressively the stock of memory—a world I come more and more to control.

So you see I am aware of the distortions I am certain to create in recollection. And to this extent my story of a day in New Brunswick, New Jersey is selective. But the facts spun themselves much as I have told. The direction, the distortion I speak of is not so much the fault of organization and form as it is the inevitable result of the additional knowledge I possess. The fact that I know the end of my story, that I later lived it—this fact forces the only intrusion or distortion my memory has so far permitted.

I do not suppose this plea separates me significantly from authors who wholly invent. For—if indeed there are such authors—they, too, may know the end of their story while they write. I draw a curious comfort, though, from my protestation. I have thus far presented material important to "character". The material digresses from the epic event of the Norfolk summer that I began by promising. And I can promise, I fear, more such digression. The comfort I take from protesting my honesty is cowardly. As I look upon these events and these people, there appears throughout an iron inevitability. It is almost as if I can say: "don't blame it on me. Life selected; life organized. My failures and stupidities, my unreason, my cruelty—these are not my fault."

A distinction here will save me some awkwardness: They are, in fact, not my fault. But they were...they were...they were...they were....

Having been exhausted by my dreams, I awoke that Saturday in Norfolk in a condition of painful fatigue. Somehow in the night my left arm had become wedged between the bedside and the wall. It was probably this trapped ache which had produced the dreams; certainly it had awakened me. For I can place my consciousness accurately at the moment when I abandoned the easy persecutions of my sleep and chose deliberately to confront the physical facts of my pain.

Karen arrived coincidentally, having risen earlier to make coffee. "Are you Ok?" she said in lieu of "good morning".

I rubbed my arm. "I guess so. Bad night."

She looked at my arm. It was red where I had rubbed it, but I do not bruise easily—there was no further mark.

"Arm hurt?" she said, kissing it.

I drew my arm back. "Yes."

She walked over to the stand where she had placed the coffee cups, picked them up gingerly, and came back to sit on the edge of the bed. I took my cup and sipped at it.

"Are you Ok?" she said. "Is the coffee Ok?"

"The coffee's fine." I said.

She looked at me for a while, I continued drinking slowly with the weight of a night's sleep laboring each careful motion. She looked at me. I thought she might be tracing each fold of my skin as I sipped, sloshed and swallowed.

"Stop watching me." I said.

She stared into her coffee. "Want a cigarette?" she said.

"Yes."

She bent to pick up the pack on the floor beside the bed. From the pack she carefully selected a cigarette, put it in her mouth, lit it, handed it to me.

"Thank you." I said.

I inhaled too deep too fast and felt a moment's dizziness, the almost fun-dizziness of a morning cigarette. I lay back and closed my eyes.

"Are you Ok?" she said,

"Yes." I said.

I opened my eyes. She was watching me again. The ash of the cigarette was too long, near dropping. My hands were at my side. Smoke curled toward my eyes, I closed them again. Karen took the cigarette from my lips to flick the ash into the tray on the floor. But the ash fell half way through her motion and disintegrated on the bed. She twisted around suddenly to brush the sheets. Her hair brushed across my face as she bent. I opened my eyes. I put my hands on her head, turning her face to me. I kissed her hard.

"Let's make love." I whispered.

I felt a moment's rigidity in her, a pause, a fraction of resistance. Then she relaxed and returned the kiss. She stretched out beside me, rubbing open the loosely tied bath robe against me.

"Are you sure?" she said.

I was sure. I caressed her, wooed her gently in silence.

"Was I too strong last night?" she said.

"Of course not." I said, and kissed her to prove it.

"You seem strange," she said.

I permitted a joke. "Just lust." I said.

She relaxed further. All was nearly well. But she could afford some more.

"I wanted you so much. Did you like it?"

"I can't remember." I said with honesty, but I smiled it into a joke. "Don't you want me now?" I added.

By now she did indeed want me. "Yes—oh yes." she said (or at least the passion equivalent), I prolonged the wooing, gently, lightly—too lightly for the passion I felt.

She managed a last try. "Was it George?" she said. "Didn't you like him?" She said it in short staccato pants like a miss-tuned radio.

My left arm crashed against the headrest. "Damn!" I said. Then, more gently, "Shut up."

She was past recognizing tone, and we made love a long long successful time.

When we were done I lit a cigarette for her. She lay back dragging deeply on the cigarette.

"You were wonderful." she said. She lay relaxed and pretty.

"I had to atone for last night." I said. I gagged on a deep swallow of cold coffee.

She felt secure enough to tease. "Just like a rabbit." she said, smiling to say "everything's fine".

I was rubbing my arm again, unconsciously. "Does it still hurt?" she said.

"Yes, it got trapped overnight."

Her eyes got scared. I smiled quickly. Her eyes stayed scared. "What's the matter?" she said.

"I hurt my goddamned arm, Ok?" I shouted. Then, because I had nothing better to do, I accidentally kicked over the cup, spilling the coffee. She jumped up to put down some Kleenex to sop up the coffee. I leaned back and looked at the room: four white bare walls, two windows, a door, a radiator, a pile of clothing, a small table-stand with a lamp, a duffle-bag, two cups (one spilled), an ashtray, a pack of cigarettes, matches, a bed, and a lovely naked girl cleaning up a mess on the floor.

Karen straightened up. The domestic chore had stiffened her posture. "I'm sorry I shouted." I said. "I had too much to drink, I guess I'm hungover."

She stood and stared at me, "You were so good." she said. "I loved you so much...you made me feel so loved."

"Come sit down." I said. "I did and I do love you." She didn't move. She looked toward the door. "I have a rehearsal this afternoon. We ought to get dressed."

I got up feeling naked and silly. The room was bare I reached for my clothes and handed her's to her. She took them and slowly, ritually began dressing.

"Karen," I said, "I don't want to go out just yet. Can't we just cuddle or something for a few minutes?"

Her face softened. We lay down together. "I want to make love," I said.

She looked surprised. "So soon?" she said, moving her hands on me for verification. Then with the nonchalance of a secure lover she removed the little clothing she had assembled. We began quickly, but this was longer than the first. Afterwards we dressed, made and drank some fresh coffee in the kitchen, and left the house.

Thus scored the Stud twice within a single morn. Thus drove he a wanton wench to the abandon of the well-spring of love. For, by his own account, each engagement was long and satisfying. Thus did she of an evening's rape gain fierce and doubled retribution—all in the name of love. And if you will characterize him as vain, arrogant, cruel—you do no more than echo my own judgment. Add to your indictment, however, Gentle Reader, that he was as well (or, perhaps, even worse) confused and unhappy. For the stud-scene did not satisfy as it might have, and he knew too well the cause of his sudden virility.

But Karen, poor girl, believed me and mistrusted her own sense of tone. Confused and (probably) unhappy, she exulted nonetheless in our flesh feast. Even I, by now, was convincing myself that my bruised arm was—if of anything—symbolic only of my disagreeably speculative mind.

Alvin

I would say now a dozen times for you that I loved her. But something even more epic than my getting it up twice occurred that day—if, that is, you will permit some slight juggling of relative time....

For had I retained consciousness that night, I would have seen the few stars go out and a deep oppressive black descend upon Norfolk.

Have you ever seen it—the New England storm? First comes the heavy darkness, crushing and scary as a graveyard on Halloween; then the small fine breeze that cuts across your face. You look toward it curiously, and then away as you sense the bite behind it. Then before you feel the change you hear the groan of its increase. Quick as the lightening it precedes, the wind snarls at you, randomly ferocious—like a hound of hell. Dust flicks at your eyes. Your hair stiffens and your breath sucks fast. For this is the lightening which you have not yet seen consolidating around you, readying for the crash. It splits the sky—the god of all glow-worms, the multi-magnification of rotting wood you can never bottle to cheer your room. The sound shakes your heart and echoes hurting through your chest. The rain begins. It hits your skin, huge and splattery, then reduces suddenly to tiny needle-pricks, multiplies them till they sting like sand. Tree limbs move grotesquely, dance, and clutch, and loudly mourn the wounded leaves bent back, split ragged.

And this is thunder-storm through the hills of New England. This is the fright, the sign, the reason of witch-burning. This is the judgment and the cause. For the new children of Eden sheltered not from Plymouth's winter, nor from Indians—but from God's wrathful thunder-rain. Towns, cities, huddled then as now, the people trembling, while vengeance filled their skies and demons, momently loosed, disported fiendishly at games too terrible to tell. The night-time storm effects no redemptive rainbow. And this was the kind of storm which, while I lay stupefied that night in

Norfolk, drove Alvin to an act of Christian charity.

He had spent the evening in Hartford, playing a pick-up job with a local dance orchestra. The storm broke upon him shortly before Canaan on the way back. For the next few miles he could see no further than a yard or two beyond his radiator. Alvin is a cautious person, timid perhaps. He cut his speed to under twenty miles-per-hour. But even this rate was too fast for his perception. As the violence of the storm increased he slowed further and considered stopping. But stopping the car entailed further risks. It was an old car and might stall if water got into the engine. Then too, could he be sure of firm ground if he pulled off the road. Some fool might smash into him if he stopped on the road, but a soft shoulder would trap him till at least morning.

Alvin was a timid person. He hated the storm, hated the decisions it was forcing upon him. Worst of all, he must decide under the intolerable circumstance of action. For stopping to think was, after all, out of the question. The act of stopping would be an act of decision.

So Alvin drove slowly, hating the storm, hoping it would go away. And then there appeared lightning flashes all around him. He had never really understood his father's talk about tires grounding a car, making it safe. Having never understood it, he had always suspected it. The sound of thunder circled, then centered on his car. He felt an insane and panic impulse to speed up, to get out of there. Near hysteria, he saw revealed in the lightening flash a man walking on the side of the road. Alvin had never picked up a hitch-hiker before. But this man was not asking for a ride; he was just walking. Somehow, moved to compassion, desperate for company, and absolved of the need to decide, Alvin stopped the car and offered a ride.

The man entered the car, "Thanks." he said.

The inside light on Alvin's car was very dim. When the door opened Alvin could not see his guest very clearly. But he saw enough to scare him. There was something about the stranger's ease—his unconcern for the storm—that troubled. And at that point the engine stalled....

Wilson

We were sitting near a tree eating our supper when Alvin told us about it. When the weather is good at Norfolk the students carry their food outside to eat sitting on the soft grassy slope beside the dining hall. There are three large elms on that gentle slope. And if you are lucky enough to get there in time you can lean your back against a tree and eat securely with the tray on your lap. If the trees are all taken you must sit Indian style — comfortable enough for ten minutes, perhaps; but soon you will put the tray beside you and stretch out lying on your side. With your nose at ant level it is not always easy to turn your head rapidly.

We were working under a system whereby Karen would bring out a tray heaped with huge helpings of everything—especially rolls and potatoes. I would gulp down what I could, then she would return for seconds. The procedure was illegal, of course; guests were supposed to pay. We grew wonderfully adept at the system, however, and only when it rained (and there was no plausible reason for eating outside) did I actually pay for a meal. The cooks must have thought it odd that Karen—a little girl, after all—could eat so much, so many potatoes and rolls. Yet they never betrayed us.

Our larcenous coup had begun that day. Later I was to get used to ducking away quickly at the approach of a school official. I would do a kind of double roll to my left, away from the food tray, and busy myself with the infinite ant-wonder of the grass world at a moment's panic. But this first afternoon it was all new to me. When Karen said, "there's Alvin", she mumbled it into her iced tea. I missed the name and violently wrenched my neck sitting up. What I saw from my new and pained perspective was a short skinny fellow with bad teeth and acne. He looked more furtive than I felt. This then was Alvin—no threat, obviously.

"It's Alvin." said Karen. "Don't look so guilty."

Alvin, who was having more trouble with her iced tea than I was, stood nervously before us, "Why should I look guilty?" he said.

"She means me." I muttered, rubbing my bruised neck with my bruised arm. "Sit down."

Alvin sat down. We were introduced.

"What's wrong with your neck?" he said.

"You made me wrench it." I said. I had meant it as a joke but, as I was to discover, Alvin had no sensitivity to tone.

"How did I do that?"

"By forcing your existence upon us."

"Oh."

"Existence precedes essence."

"Are you kidding?"

"No, I am irrevocably serious."

"Well...I didn't mean to...."

"Of course you didn't. You can't help being what you are."

"I mean, I didn't mean to intrude."

"Well you did."

"No, I didn't. Intrude, I mean."

"Oh."

Karen began laughing hysterically and truth suddenly broke upon Alvin. He grinned shyly and began to stir the cup of coffee he had been slopping all over while performing the manual of apology.

"I'm sorry." I said. "My humor has been called destructive."

"I'm sure I'd have understood...." Alvin said. He paused to drink some coffee. He lowered his nose to where the level had been. But most of the coffee had spilled out. He looked surprised. Above the rim of the cup his eyes appeared to dart suddenly toward the remaining coffee. With a quick bird-like jerk he buried his nose further in the cup and drank. "I guess they're rationing it." he said.

He continued, "You see, I'm sure I'd have understood you were joking and all, but I had a very strange night."

And then he told us about his ride and the storm....

When the car stalled the stranger said, "I'll take care of it." He got out of the car and walked to the front where he raised the hood and began doing something to the engine. Alvin sat petrified. Lightening was flashing all about the car, but still he had not seen the stranger's face. It was, he thought, no doubt the drama of the storm; but was there not something ominous in the phrase, "I'll take care of it"? His vulnerable fancy caught the words and twisted them to a dozen shapes while he waited to be murdered or struck down by God's heavenly fire—or worse.

Alvin did not smoke, but suddenly he wished desperately for a cigarette. It occurred to him that his roommate's jacket might be in the back seat. Bill had driven the car earlier that day, and he often left clothes in the back seat. Once, to his acute embarrassment, Alvin had found some girls' underwear in the back seat. He had often (insofar as he ever lectured) asked Bill to not, please, leave clothing in the back seat. Despite or because of his acne, Alvin had a passion for order.

But the storm, which previously had only demoralized him, had now disorganized him to the point where he thought there just might be a pack of cigarettes in the jacket that just might be in the back seat. Alvin turned to reach his hand over to the back. There was nothing on the seat but an oily rag he had used to clean the windshield. He thought possibly the jacket that might be in the back seat might have fallen to the floor. He straightened up and stretched his body around and over to sweep the floor with his fingers. His head was now vertical and below his belly on which he balanced, hanging from the top of the front seat—his feet hooked under the steering-wheel for leverage. He was in this position when the stranger opened the door.

A flash of lightening burst upon them as Alvin jumped back to the driver's seat, hitting the horn as he did so. It was one of those long bright day-sky flashes and, even in his present confusion, Alvin was able to get a good look at his guest. The stranger was dressed completely in black. He was about seven feet tall, muscular, lean and savage. He wore a weather-beaten Stetson. His face was unshaven and he had a long dark moustache after the fashion of Fu Manchu.

"What are you doing?" he asked.

All of Alvin's circuits were open, and up and down his nervous system was relayed each possible (and impossible) explanation, along with its attendant qualification. Alvin has little sense of self-absurdity. But he is timid, and like most timid persons he knows what other people are inclined to think absurd. And something peculiar happened to him at this moment. With his life at stake before this sinister stranger, Alvin's backbone stiffened. After all, he thought, the cigarette pack might well have fallen down through the crack in the seat.

"I was looking for a cigarette." He announced fearlessly.

The stranger sat down on the seat beside Alvin and closed the door. Lightening coiled around the periphery, refracted and blazed from the metal studs of what looked like a motorcycle jacket. The stranger turned toward Alvin. A greased hand glided purposefully into the side pouch of the jacket—the diagonal slash pocket. The hand produced a pack of cigarettes.

"Have one of mine." Said the stranger.

Betrayed by twenty-three years of habit, Alvin replied: "No thanks, I don't smoke."

There was a pause. Then the stranger said, "Try the starter; I've fixed it."

Alvin pushed the starter and the engine came to life....

Shane

And that was the tale Alvin told us while we ate our supper that Saturday night in Norfolk. Alvin had stammered through it, apologetic, earnest—that personal tone he always assumed. And, though I soon grew to loathe it, on this first meeting I thought I had never heard anything quite so funny. Karen lay back on the grass, shaking helplessly. And even Alvin, who has a partial retrospective sense of humor, smiled shyly.

"Well," I said, finally, "what happened?"

"Oh, he didn't have a place to stay, so I put him up on the couch."

"After all that?" said Karen.

"Well what could I do? It was raining and all...."

"You're wonderful." said Karen. "What's he here for? Is he just bumming around?"

"No." Alvin said. He paused uncomfortably. "He says he knows someone here."

"Who?" I said.

"I don't know," said Alvin, "I know this sounds maybe funny, but I didn't like to ask him anything. He told me a lot about himself...."

"Who told who a lot?" said George, who had just come upon us.

I essayed some calm and did not even turn to look at him. Karen turned quickly. I was lying on my side, watching her, and I saw her turn quickly and smile.

"Alvin has a sinister friend," she laughed. "He came last night in the thunderstorm."

George squatted beside me and braced a fraternal hand on my shoulder.

"Hi, George." I smiled at him. "It seems Alvin has a mysterious stranger."

Alvin shifted his feet. He looked at us and then shifted his feet again. A shyness had come upon him that even he seemed unused to. Possibly he did not dare risk a re-telling. A confident raconteur might hesitate to perform twice before the same audience. With less grace than usual, he stood up.

"I've got to go." he apologized. "You tell him about it."

"But what did he say?" said Karen, "about himself?"

Alvin shrugged. "I don't know." he said. "He seems like a nice enough guy."

Alvin was swinging his arms, walking backwards away from us. Then he realized he had forgotten his coffee cup. He came back and stooped down to pick it up. The spoon fell off the saucer on to the grass. Without completely squatting, Alvin tried to sweep up the spoon with his free hand. Off-balance, he jerked back a little, and the coffee cup slid off the saucer he was holding in his other hand.

Our reactions were different, and it might be profitable to suspend time for the moment to relate them: Alvin was, of course, simply a structure of awkwardness and embarrassment. I watched with sadistic fascination. I had never before seen any human figure so grotesquely posed. His right knee was flexed at about a sixty-degree angle, twisted to the right in a direct line with the spoon, one end of which still touched the grass. The handle of the spoon was, appropriately enough, in his hand, outstretched on a line from his extended arm. But the line formed by his arm and hand was all wrong for the intersection with the line of his knee. If a center point could be calculated, Alvin had missed it by several inches. It was, I would have guessed, impossible for an arm and a leg to be pointed at each other, at that angle, to any constructive use. The extra step he should have taken before he bent now assumed, by its absence, a large—though not entirely serious—significance. Not only was his left side out of control, but he was trying to balance himself on the spoon! The ground was soft, for it had rained the night before. As the spoon sank, so did Alvin—flailing wildly, sprawling on his right side.

Karen was laughing. I was observing with wonder and awe. George sank forward to his knees. He deftly took the saucer from Alvin's falling hand, and caught the cup in mid-air with the hand he had been fraternally bracing on my shoulder. It was a neat bit of juggling and we appreciated it.

Alvin scrambled up and took the cup and saucer from George.

"Artist's hands." said Karen.

"No," George smiled, "ping-pong hands."

"He plays ping-pong." said Alvin over his shoulder. He was walking down the hill again.

"What's his name?" called Karen.

Alvin was at the driveway now. "Wilson." he shouted. "His name's Wilson."

"Stark Wilson?" I laughed. But Alvin had dropped his spoon again, and could not hear me.

George sat down and we stared after Alvin, the three of us smiling and silent. The sun was now low in the sky. I lay back and watched the mountains change color. A light breeze moved a cloud or two across the hills. All was clear and fresh as the after-wash of a summer shower. We sat together silently for some time. My thoughts were of form and color. Like many another writer, my sense of art is limited, wistful, and rather old-fashioned. I was wishing I could paint a landscape. The wish was near my tongue when Karen began chuckling.

"What is it?" I said sharply. I was afraid she had read my thinking.

"Stark Wilson." she said. "I just caught it. Sinister stranger... Stark Wilson." And she laughed again.

"What's that?" said George.

"In Shane." I said. "Stark Wilson is the villain in Shane...the movie... you know."

George grinned. "Shane, too?" He shook his head. "You know, I thought I was the only one left who remembered Shane. That's a great movie. But I don't remember Wilson had a first name."

"He doesn't." I said. "That's in the novel."

"There's a novel?"

"Yes."

"I didn't know that."

"Jack Schaefer." said Karen proudly. "You see, there are three of us."

"Stark Wilson..." said George. "Yes...that fits. Remember how he rides in...?"

And we all three remembered....

Dawn...the broad flat plains of Wyoming...the sinister black figure riding his pale horse with sensual feline grace...determined... inexorable... into town...camera from within Grafton's saloon...close-up of the face of Jack Palance...Stark Wilson...masked by the top of the swinging doors...the doors burst inward...camera to the black boots...up the brown clad legs... to the deadly black guns...Stark Wilson...standing proud...menacing... dwarfing the screen....

"The dog..." I said. "The dog...."

Within the saloon the few idlers freeze...Wilson scans the room slowly...cool eyes noting detail...a dog gets up and slinks belly-low in fright across the room...Riker has sold his soul...Wilson drinks only coffee...black gloved hand hooking around the cup like a predatory claw...the eyes above the rim of the cup never cease looking...never cease....

We laughed. Karen hissed, and we laughed again.

"Remember?" she said. She looked at me shyly....

It had been our first date. Karen and I had eaten at a restaurant where she had told me of the free movies at The Ledge.

"What's playing?" I said.

"Shane. It's a western."

"Shane. It's my favorite movie."

"Haven't they made one of The Duchess?"

"OK, OK. But let's go. How far is it? Do we have time?"

"Yes...is it really that good? I thought it was just a western."

"Baby," I said, "Shane is the ultimate western. It's a medieval morality play."

"Well," she said, "I suppose that's good," And we hurried off....

It is good. And though I suppose there are few of my generation who ever enjoyed it without embarrassment, Shane is the Great American Movie.

Telling movies is a weakness I have never outgrown. And it is, I suppose, a silly weakness. For movies are visual, not literary, and Shane is among the most visual of all. In those days of Karen and George and Norfolk, I would act out movies when I told them: crouching to point camera angles, standing tall, legs spread, for Wilson's taunting challenge; posing in slow-motion, still, for Starret's dramatic entrance to save Shane—the ax-handle angled just right to come crashing through the door into the faces of my audience. All these were necessary to my telling and I did them well—for how else could the movie be explained? You had to see exactly how far Torrey's gun is out of the holster when he hears Shipstead's warning and realizes that Wilson's gun is ready—that he is about to die. You had to see exactly how Torrey hesitates, in order to realize the evil of Wilson's act. It is murder. But you had to see it, and then see Wilson smile as Torrey's body is blasted into the mud he had been so carefully stepping over, moments before.

Now I am less vigorous, though perhaps wiser, and I write critical essays and plot summaries. For, after all, anyone can see the film, and many have already done so. If you recall Shane reasonably well I do not insist that you read the following—for it is only summary. The interpretation that comes later may also be passed, perhaps to advantage, if you see the film—and I think I had rather you saw it. But such interpretation contains, at least, some flavor of my younger self, and what I thought of Shane might conceivably interest you. The following summary, however, partakes of no such self-indulgence, and, consequently, seems to me not very interesting—though I can hardly proceed without it:

Shane, a blond, buckskin-clad gunman with a gentle smile and a past, rides into the valley where there is a conflict for possession of the range between Riker, the rancher, and the farmers, led by Joe Starret. Shane, no farmer, allies himself with Starret, taking the job of hired handy-man. Told by Starret to avoid conflict, Shane refuses to fight when taunted in Grafton's Saloon. This refusal is taken for cowardice. Shane loses face with Starret's boy, Joey, and the other farmers. Shane returns to the saloon and provokes the fight, readily defeating Chris Galloway, the taunter. Riker offers Shane a job. Shane refuses. Riker suggests Shane desires Starret's wife, Marian. Shane insults him. Riker orders his men to beat Shane. Shane fights well but is overcome. Joey, observing all, calls his father. Starret enters with an ax-handle. He and Shane defeat the group. Riker is furious and sends for a hired killer, Wilson. At the Fourth of July celebration Wilson is described to Shane. Shane appears to have heard of him. That night Riker visits Starret's home to attempt a compromise. Starret will not desert the other farmers. While they debate the issue, Shane and Wilson examine each other with apparent recognition. The next day Wilson provokes a hot-headed farmer, Torrey, into a gun-fight, and kills him. The killing nearly stampedes the farmers, but Starret and Shane rally them at Torrey's funeral—aided by Riker's precipitous action, setting fire to the house of a farmer. Riker decides he must kill Starret, and sends an invitation for a meeting in town. Chris Calloway, reformed, warns Shane that Starret will be facing Wilson as well as Riker. Shane puts on his gun and tells Starret not to go. Starret protests it is his duty. They fight. Shane clubs Starret with a gun. Shane prepares for the show-down and says good-by to Marian....

"And it was a year before I ever knew how it came out." Karen laughed.

We were walking, the three of us, up the path toward the "barn". Karen had left some sheet-music in one of the practice rooms. On the lawn by the Administration building (called, for obvious reasons, the "White House") some people were playing croquet. George and I stopped to watch while Karen went on up ahead.

"Tell him." she called back. "Tell him why. He'll appreciate it."

George looked at me. "Go ahead." he smiled.

I looked out at the croquet players. One was preparing for a long shot. He was studying the grass with all the fine concentration of a golf professional. The wicket was at least fifty feet distant from him, and the lawn, though close-cut, was uneven. I watched him practise-swing the mallet while his partner shouted encouragement. George was watching me waiting.

"Well..." I said. That day had been important to me....

Movie Night

We arrived at The Ledge five minutes before the movie began. Already the crowd was clapping rhythmically. The lights were still on. We hurried past the reception desk and down the short stairs to the large auditorium. At one end of the hall a large screen had been set up precariously on a wooden table. Several stuffed lounge chairs had been turned to face the screen. The rest of the auditorium had been filled with set-up folding chairs. We paused at the bottom step, searching the room for a seat. There were about three hundred people already packed in, and more circulating on the sides. The noise was increasing. Karen held tight to my arm. Across the room a hand waved to me. It was JD, we started across toward him. At my third step I tripped on a bottle and almost fell. I straightened immediately, annoyed and unhurt. I assured Karen I was all right. She stood close to me.

"I've never seen it so bad." she said. She had to shout. We got to JD. Miraculously he had an extra seat, and helped me take another from two rows down.

"Thought you might make it...." he said, "Shane and all."

"Is it always like this?" I said.

"Fraternity parties tonight, and they're getting a head start."

The lights dimmed to great applause. We relaxed back in our chairs. A center aisle had been carved for the projector. I was on that aisle, with the side-light of the projector glaring over my right shoulder. Karen was to my left, JD beyond her.

There was an amoeba of light, off-center, on the screen; then more applause and shouting while it was being adjusted. I could hear the table groan beside me as it was moved. Then on the screen appeared the fuzzy legend: "George Stevens presents Shane". It focused even before the protests, and the credits began. The sound-track had not yet started, but there was promising static from the sides of the hall.

Remarks went their predictable rounds—Jack Palance (his first movie?) listed "Walter Jack Palance". But the music finally started and things were settling down. JD leaned past Karen to ask me was A.B. Guthrie Jr. any relation to Woody. I chuckled at him and waited for the movie, leaning forward in my seat to see the opening shot.

Shane appeared in living Technicolor, the camera at his back and over his right shoulder as he began riding down out of the beautiful Wyoming mountains. My breath quickened. And then the film broke and the music ground down rasping. The lights were on and the audience was cheering again.

Keren whispered in my ear, "When does the Duchess ride in?"

I laughed at her.

"No," she smiled, "really...when?"

"What?" said JD. He was leaning over her.

"She said, when does the Duchess ride in?" I told him.

"Duchess?"

"Of Malfi." said Karen, squeezing my hand.

"Oh." he said. "You don't waste much time."

"Neither do you." I reminded him. But he chose not to understand.

"It's not really a western, is it?" said Karen. "I mean, they'll start playing ping-pong or something, won't they?"

"OK, OK." I said. I put my arms over my head. "I talk too much."

She put her head against my shoulder. I drew my left arm around her, accidentally brushing someone's arm behind me. "Sorry." I said over my shoulder,

"'s OK, man, get shum for me too" was the answer. I ignored him. The lights went out again, and the film started. It stuttered for a second or two, and then began.

Shane continued down out of the mountains. He was beautiful in clean buckskins and a white Stetson. His horse was plain, brown and white, and he rode it easily. I settled back.

A deer crossed a pool of water, and behind it, a boy, Joey, was stalking, holding a rifle—unloaded, as I knew. Close-up of Joey's face. Then the deer turned and saw Shane far in the distance. It raised its head and stared for a moment, then loped off. Joey turned to look at what the deer had seen, and then watched carefully, excitedly.

Each viewing taught me something new. Now for the first time I noticed the opening motion from animal to boy to man. For the camera turned to Joe Starret, hard at work chopping at the stump outside his cabin. Joe Starret—farmer—clearing the land. "Someone's coming, Pa." said Joey. Starret paused in his labor to survey the road. He looked at the distant horseman calm and steady. "Well—let him come," he said, wiping his brow and returning to the stump.

Karen stirred beside me. She had caught the line and was excited by it.

"Mind if I cut through your land?" said Shane.

Starret paused, "No, I guess not." he answered thoughtfully.

"I didn't expect to see any fences up this way." said Shane as he guided his horse carefully through the yard. Shane leaned forward to speak to Joey: "You were watching me quite a ways down the road, weren't you? I like a man that keeps his eyes open. It means he'll make his mark." Joey grinned shyly. So did I.

Starret offered water and Shane dismounted. Joey broke open his rifle. At the sound Shane whirled around into a crouch, his hand at his gun. Clean buckskin—friendly—kind—but a gunman and a past.

The audience laughed and cheered, obliterating Starret's comment and Marian's opening line. Karen leaned forward impatiently. The crowd roared again as again the reel broke.

"What did she say?" said Karen.

"You know better than to point guns at people." I told her. "Then Joey says, I wasn't pointing it at any one, Mother."

To my right some frantic activity was going on. Hands worked at the projector, flickering the aide-light across my face. The audience began the rhythmic applause. JD leaned toward me. "Here," he said, passing me a flask, "might be a long night. Might as well get in the spirit."

I took a small sip and passed the flask back to Karen. She took a drink.

"Thass it, man, " said the voice behind me, "thass the way. Get shum for me too."

I looked back at him, but was blinded by the light from the projector. "OK!" I said savagely. "Enough!"

"Shhh..." said several people near me. The film had begun again.

Starret heard Riker's men coming and, snatching Joey's rifle, turned on Shane, ordering him off the farm. "Put down the rifle." Said Shane. "Then I'll go."

"What's the difference?" said Starret. "You're leaving anyway."

"I'd like it to be my idea." said Shane.

There were some cheers and a reacting shushing sound throughout. There were allies in the audience, though I could not see them past the darkness and the light of the projector.

And now Riker's men were humiliating Starret, bullying, trampling his garden. And everyone was silent with indignation. Until around the corner of the cabin, gently, smoothly sliding into the right-hand corner of the screen—was Shane, taking his stand. "I'm a friend of Starret's."

And many people cheered at this. And I tried to look past the light again—because I was confused, and had almost cheered, myself.

Then Riker's men had left, and Starret turned in embarrassment to apologize to Shane, and to introduce himself and his family. Shane shook his hand, smiling. "You can call me Shane."

It warmed me for a second. But a voice at the front yelled, "Call him Shane." And here and there the answer grated: "Shane." "Shane."

Karen whispered to me, "Look you, the Starrets shine still."

"Jesus!" I said.

I was impressed. I was impressed by her wit and I just sat there. "Jesus." I said again.

She thought she had offended me. "I'm sorry." She whispered. "I'll be good."

"No," I turned to her. "You are good." And I kissed her lightly.

"Thass it, man," cried The Voice, "get shum for me too."

But he was shushed before I had to act, for a new pressure group was making its strength felt now. And for a time power seemed to hang in even balance between good and evil. And the only problem was that the flicker was confusing me, and the shushing sound reminded me of nothing so much as a drunken snake.

I laughed a little at the idea and at myself. I was beginning to feel good-humored about the whole rowdy business, when I realized that Starret was explaining his theory of modern farming. I suddenly recollected the naivety of the next words and shrank into my chair, cowering till the line hit:

"...why, he'll make out." said Starret. He looked to Marian. "We make out, don't we?"

The ripples fanned out from giggle to belly-laugh. Ready though I was, the breath was struck from me by the heavy slap on my back. It was my unseen adversary behind me, sharing his joke with me again. I was paralyzed. It was Karen who turned to him and said: "Thass right, man." Wonderful girl!

But Shane hangs in a balance as fine as the audience's—myth, plot and naturalism. And when Starret and Shane defeat seven of Riker's men... when they back out slowly, victoriously, with Starret's war cry about the damages...when the music swells proud, triumphant.... Yet response is self-perpetuating and gets out of control. At Riker's "gunsmoke" line there was a brief commotion near the back of the auditorium. I saw three Campus Patrolmen rushing down the stairs. I shook off JD's flask and covered my right eye. I could believe none of it. Whatever I should or should not do seemed pre-determined, I flickered in an ambiguous ripple somewhere near the balance. The center held and the film went on and on.

They hissed Wilson, but they laughed at Marian. They gasped at Torrey's death, but they mocked his funeral. And then Shane and Starret were fighting each other—brutal, savage, while the horses plunged and kicked, and Marian, her view partially frustrated by the horses, looked from one to the other of the two men she loved equally—and held her head and shrieked. Then, back against the stump, the up-rooting of which had begun their alliance, Shane drew his gun and struck Starret to the ground.

Shane and Marian said good-by, tender, under-stated. "And you're never coming back?" she said. "Never's a long time." said Shane. They looked at each other, long, longing. "Shane", she said. There was an awkward pause. Finally, she held out her hand. "Take care of yourself, Shane." she said as he shook her hand.

The guy behind me laughed, coarse, brutal: "Haw haw haw." and the balance suddenly shifted, propelling me up and out of my chair. "Stand up!" I screamed, and threw myself at him before he could.

There was a clatter of falling chairs, and both of us were on the floor. I had somehow managed to hit him and he was moaning. There were shouts and crunchings all around me. I got to my feet. He was whining, "Why'd you have to do that, man?" He was grabbing at my feet. I couldn't bring myself to kick him. I stepped back. There was more crashing near me and shrieking and confusion. Someone was yelling for lights. And someone else—it was JD—was calling my name. I stepped back again and fell heavily against the table. Strobe light shot past my left side as my shoulder began falling with the projector. There was an apocalyptic detonation and no light. My shoulder and back felt broken.

I lay still, fearing I was broken. I could hear riot screams and the thud of fists. I lay still. And then a couple of people were on me, hitting me, and I rolled to one side, fighting at them weakly. My breath caught. I was being strangled. I flailed at the assassin, but he was not material—only his hands choking me, tightening on my throat. Then there were lights, and JD was pulling at my throat, ripping away the film I had rolled up in. I began to understand and tore at it myself. He helped me up. I saw him fling the metal wheel at someone near. I sprinted for the stairs.

Then I remembered Karen, I looked around the hall. Couples were streaming out the exits on all sides. The center of the floor seethed with motion, a weird and nightmare fluid. "Here." Karen called. She was holding the broken end of a stand-up lamp near the top step. I raced up the steps. "JD." I said. I took the lamp from her and started back. There was a roar from the front as the screen pitched forward, crackling thunder as it folded on itself. Below it, a row of chairs was thrown backward, the clatter muffled by softer collisions of scrambling panicked flesh, and the shrill shrieks of the nearly-smothered. I paused, fascinated. Thunder diminished ludicrously to fabric, a soft tearing zipper sound, as a head appeared through the screen—the popped terrified eyes inviting either the revolution pike or a well-aimed custard pie. I was struck and spun to the

side. An army of Campus Police was racing past me down into the mob,
I staggered back and saw JD. JD had seen the police, and was climbing
up the side of the shelf near the stairs. He waved to us, and slung a leg
over the top. Below, the police were dragging on the motion at the center.
JD laughed wildly and stood on the top of the bannister. His laugh shot
across the roar and plunged like a hawk to the boiling stream below.

"Riker ain't payin for this damage! Not a nickel" he cried out to the auditorium. "I'm payin for what's broke. No, by Godfrey! Me and Shane—
we are payin for what's broke!"

"Good Night, Shane"

...the croquet ball was near the wicket now. It seemed on target, but losing speed. From our position it would have been hard to calculate. But one of the opponents stepped in front of the wicket and clubbed the ball away before we could tell. There was a cry of rage from the partner of the man who had made the shot. The partner of the man who had clubbed it away called out immediately, "Beautiful shot! We concede." His partner laughed and nodded. The man who had made the shot leaned on his mallet and said nothing.

"Well...." I said. "It was a student showing. There was a fight and the projector was broken before the end of the film."

I lit a cigarette. George said nothing.

"It was a rowdy crowd." I said, "And I got mad at some comments. There was a fight. It was our first date."

"Quite a beginning." he said. He turned toward the "barn" where Karen could now be seen returning up the path. She waved to us.

"Yes." I said. "It was."

"Did you tell him?" said Karen.

"Yes," I said. I smiled maliciously. "Everything."

She affected a blush and put her free arm around me. "I hope not." she said. She smiled at George, "What do you think of my hero?" she asked him.

Whatever he thought was interrupted by Benny, the Art Director, who was passing us on the path. Benny is a tall man with the ratty, pop-eyed face of a dissipated young English lord. He is as mean as his face, as petty as his moustache. He has never been known to speak a civil word. As he passed us, he spoke to George out of the side of his mouth:

"The loft is a fire-trap. Get those boys to straighten up."

"It's Saturday night." George said pleasantly enough to the receding back.

Benny did not turn at once. But he stopped. "What?" he said.

"I said it's Saturday night." George said, "I may not be able to find them."

"Then do it yourself." said Benny. "That's what you're paid for."

"He's kidding!" Karen whispered loudly.

Benny walked back to us. His moustache quivered a bit. "I am not kidding, young lady." he said. "And while we're on the subject...." He paused and glowered at George.

"All right," George said, still pleasantly, "I'll see to it."

Benny turned and walked off. Karen trembled. "That sonofabitch!" she said.

"You have to understand," George smiled, "power corrupts. Come on. It looks like I may be a while. Why don't you two play ping-pong while I see what has to be done."

We started toward the "barn".

"I thought I'd escaped all that." I muttered.

"Oh," George said, "the Army. Like a sergeant?"

"No. They're OK. It's the officers..." I began.

"But they're like you." said Karen.

"Bull shit.'" I said, "They're like nobody but pricks with striped pants."

We walked in silence, I was angry.

"Is it like this often?" I asked.

"No." he said. "Not like you...not every day. Just when he's upset. You see, well...think why painters become administrators. The Yale System — it's beautifully logical. It gets the kids painting like Deans. Or it would. They practise the System, but they listen to me, too. It makes for friction...," He broke off, "Benny's OK. Think what it must be like, having it all except talent.... Here, I'll go round up my sloppy geniuses while you play."

He went up the stairs to the loft. Karen and I began to hit the ball. It felt good playing with her again. I was a bit rusty, but I warmed to the play. She was playing well. Her timing was excellent, and she seemed to be hitting harder than usual. I complimented her.

"Oh, I've been playing a lot." she said. "Are you ready for a game?"

I thought so. She won the service and began. Her first two serves were conventional to her play: a vigorous tennis-type body wind-up, followed by a disproportionately gentle serve—three-quarter speed, but comfortably high. Her third serve, however, surprised me, and tied me up. It was harder, and low.

"Good serve." I said.

"Thanks." she said, and served another. It was even harder, and toward my backhand. Karen had never before been able to adjust the direction of her serve very accurately. Though I returned it, the return was weak and high. She hesitated, considered slamming; but thought better and placed it instead—not a good placement, and I nearly put it away. But I was still off form, and missed the table. She retrieved the ball.

"That's quite a serve." I said.

She grinned. "I've been saving it for you. George taught it to me."

He hadn't, actually. It was no more than a modification of one of my own serves I had shown her years before. But she had managed to get comfortable with it.

She served again. But she hit it too hard and off the table. "Pressure." she said ruefully. "I just can't think about it."

I served and missed a few. She was way ahead when George leaned around the stair railing.

"This is going to be quite a project." He said. "When you've had enough, go on without me. I'll see you later. Casey's?"

"OK." Said Karen. "Hey, I'm winning."

"Good girl." He said.

"It's your serve." I said to him.

"Good, but you'll never beat him." He went back upstairs.

"Maybe I will." Said Karen.

I shook my head. "Pressure." I said.

And, inevitably, as I became sharper the point spread narrowed.

At fifteen-all, Karen paused, "Hey, what am I doing wrong?"

"You're playing better than ever." I said. "You've just forgotten how good I am."

"No." she said. "I don't think I've forgotten. I don't know...somehow I just don't make it."

She tightened her whole body and served hard. I barely returned it, but she let the advantage pass and I took the point.

I told her, as I had a hundred times, "You don't have a slam. You can't win without a slam."

"George can." She retorted. "He doesn't slam."

As she spoke, she served again. I lobbed it over, high to her backhand. The ball hung insultingly easy. She fell back, off-balance, to belt it over her shoulder in that wild reverse haymaker that always seemed so eccentric. It landed, however, and I wasn't ready for it. The next two serves I lobbed back the same, and she swung wildly at each, missing.

"One-out-of-three." I said. "Give it up, Karen."

She glared at me. "Can't you see..." she snarled, "can't you see that's my slam? I have to take a chance. It would be nothing...my game would be nothing without that. It's my style. You talk about style all the time. That's my style."

"Let's quit." I said.

She drew a breath. "No...I'm sorry. You're right, I lose...but that's not all. I must be doing something else."

"Pressure." I laughed. It didn't score.

"I win a few games." she said. She was not smiling. "Look." She point-ed to a paper taped to the wall near the water cooler. I looked at the paper. It was a tournament listing, Karen had placed fifth; George had won. Be-side the list was another—a rating list. Karen was third; George was first again.

"I'm not surprised." I said. "You're playing awfully well. That's good, though, fifth out of thirty. That's wonderful."

She relaxed suddenly. She stood beside me. "Well," she said, "it was pressure, I guess. In spite of the tournament, they still think I'm third best."

"That must bug Mr. Three and Four," I said.

"I should have beat them anyway. But, you know, I did win a game with that shot—the one you don't like. It was 20-19, and I just made up my mind to make it—and I did.... I'm sorry I'm a grouch."

Ah, Karen—I thought—you won that game with twenty other shots. But I did not say so. I knew enough to nuzzle her hair. She stepped back and looked at me shyly.

"What is it?" she said. "Why aren't I better?"

"Karen," I said, "you're the best."

"No. You know...."

"You lack ruthlessness," I said, "the killer instinct. Thank God."

She pushed back her hair. "Wait till you play George. He's the most detached player you'll ever see."

(I should explain that Karen actually pushes her hair forward, that is, over her ears and to the front—a mannerism I must take credit for, since it results from my habit of tucking her hair back behind her ears.)

"Maybe that's what I mean." I spoke thoughtfully.

"Not if you mean you." she said. "I can't imagine two more different styles. And you look so much alike...."

"Well, let's get a beer." I said. And we walked down the long path to Casey's.

But Casey's was crowded, and the waitress gave us trouble about age identification. (She was a sour little creature who made a point of demanding identification of forty year olds if she thought they belonged to the school). At the end of one beer apiece, I asked Karen if we couldn't go on home. "Where is it, by the way?" I added.

"What?"

"Home."

"I thought we'd stay at George's, OK? We have a room to ourselves—practically the whole house."

"Won't he mind if we just take over?"

"He's not like that." she said.

"What is he like?" I said.

She grinned at me. "Puzzled, aren't you? The mirror thing. He's like you—can't you tell?"

We were on the grass slope before his house. I reached down and picked a few blades of grass which I pressed to her cheek. The grass was damp and cool. She drew back and giggled, pushing my hand away. A droplet glistened on her cheek and she brushed it off.

"Now you're attacking me with grass." she said. "It's like the ice-cubes."

We had this private joke that she feared ice-cubes and I was curing her, forcing her to face her fear by attacking her with ice-cubes. This was what she referred to, and why she giggled. But her retraction was involuntary, and may have had a different source.

Of course, I began this epic by declaring that a spilled cigarette ash contained secrets of life. No doubt the bare form of such a declaration mitigates against belief, puts (as an old teacher of mine used to say) the reader on his guard. Yet that was, in total, a pompous page. And the sheer weight of its weariness may have made my saws bearable. I am not now so young even as when I began this tale. And since much of it is strange, I will solicit belief where I can—even at the expense of such wisdoms as I might reveal. Therefore, I shall not insist on the significance of a blade of grass. Rather, I will baldly explain that she had missed my meaning.

"No." I said. "Don't you remember?"

She looked at me, puzzled for a moment. I scuffed at the grass and kicked up a divot, which I failed to replace.

"Oh." she said, and nodded as we entered George's house.

The front room did not seem to me as large as it had seemed the night before—a peculiar inversion of normal relativity. Nor were the front stairs as high as I had thought. As we ascended them, I paused for a moment, trying to recollect something. I found it, and we went to our room.

Darkness seemed to have softened the outlines, and the light at the bed which Karen turned on lengthened rather velvety shadows across the window-side. Then I noticed the reason: curtains had been hung at the windows.

They were an artistic inspiration—a fact I realized within seconds. For, on the outside, they were splashed in gay patterns with vivid color streaks. Yet on the inside—that area exposed by the light of the bed-lamp—the curtains appeared solid blue, elegant, the proper shadow color and form. Sunlight would brighten the room, not dazzle it hospital color; night caused a gentle blue sleep-calm. An inspiration.

"He hasn't wasted any time." I said.

"Yes." she nodded. "I guess he means for us to stay."

"Nice of him, anyway," I said.

She nodded, and began undressing. I sat on the bed, watching her.

"A little." I said.

"What?" She was emerging from beneath her slip.

"A little like me, I guess."

"What?"

"George, I suppose he is a little like me."

"A lot."

"Yes, perhaps. Yet there are differences...." I bit at my lip meditatively. "There was something I wanted to ask you, but I can't...."

"What?" she said. She had been smothered in a night-gown which she was now smoothing out against her body.

"There's something I wanted to ask you." I repeated. "But I can't remember."

"Oh." she said. She put her hand to her face, "Oh! I forgot to tell you something. They've requisitioned the car for tomorrow. It's some darned brass concert, but I'll have to drive. We'll be gone all day. If you want to come.... but I thought maybe you'd like to wander around a little and see the place."

She crossed the room and came into the bed. I began taking off my shoes.

"No," I said. "It's all right, I want some time anyway. I've got a story going. Maybe I can do some work on it tomorrow."

"Good," She smiled. "Is it good?"

"I can't tell yet."

I undressed quickly and turned off the light. Shadows, cast from a streetlight far outside still formed about the curtains and the room.

"I'll bet it is." Karen said. "You're both artists. I mean your stories and his curtains."

I sat up and made a recollection sound.

"What?" she said.

"The song." I said. "The song Ross was playing. What is it?"

"I don't know. What song?"

"Something about green green rocky road."

"That's it." she said. "That's what it's called.... no, it's "promenade in green"...but I don't remember him singing it last night."

"Perhaps I imagined it. How does the tune go?"

"You couldn't imagine it if you don't know it." She softly hummed it for me. She has a lovely voice, low and sweet. I picked up the tune and whispered it to myself, I could hear it clearly in my head.

She laughed gently. "When are you going to learn, silly; you can't whisper a tune. There's no difference in pitch when you whisper."

"But I can hear it." I muttered.

"You'll never make a musician." she sighed.

"But I did," I said, "you."

"All right," she growled, "enough of that...are you sleepy?"

"Yes."

"So am I. Would you mind...?"

"Of course not. It's been a long day."

"I'm sorry about tomorrow."

"It's OK. Really. I'll work."

"Good."

I lay back for a while and sang softly to myself:

Green green rocky road

Promenade In green

Tell me who you love....

Karen turned to me. "You." she said, taking my hand. "You."

I held her hand but I hummed the refrain again:

Green green rocky road

Promenade in green

Tell me who you love

Tell me who you love

Green green rocky road

Promenade in green....

"Dick," she said, "hold me. Don't say anything—just hold me." I held her till she fell asleep.

But sleep did not come to me for a long while. I lay back and watched the shadows flicker. Now and then a truck would haul up the steep incline through Norfolk. Its lights would dodge past the curtains and search the far wall, then vanish with the rumbling of the labored engine as it passed the house. More interesting, perhaps, were the shadows driven before the light. They would appear from nowhere, distend, and writhe along the wall. Then as they grew longer thinner, they would strike the door and vanish. Sometimes they seemed to slip through the crack of the door and escape to the hall. Sometimes, depending, I suppose, on how far to the center of the road the truck made its turn—sometimes they would appear merely to die at the door.

I watched them for a long time, and then closed my eyes. Some things connected randomly and I began to put them into order. The bed was soft and large enough for two to rest comfortably. I lay there floating freely in the balance of my thought.

Considering the day I had spent, I do not now wonder that my meditation turned to Shane:

The lamp and the shadows of the Starrets' cottage. Joe retires off to the right. Shane and Marian look at each other. She offers to bandage his head. Shane assures her that he is all right. Joey calls to her to tell her something. She goes to his room and, while they whisper, Shane slowly gets up and goes out the cabin door to the barn. Joey's whispers are loud enough to hear clearly; Marian's answers are barely audible. "Mother, I just love Shane...I love him almost as much as I do Pa. That's all right, isn't it?" "Yes, dear, that's, all right." If Shane has heard, he gives no indication. Marian returns to the room and stares out the door-window after him. The camera has not moved. The action is smooth, under-stated, and re-mote. Starret enters the room, dressed in his long underwear. "What's the matter?" he says. "Joe," she says, "hold me. Don't say anything—just hold me." And he does, patting her affectionately—cumbersome hands, honest hands. They walk off-camera into their room, arm in arm. The camera does not move. There is no person on the screen. Joey whispers loudly from his room. "Good night. Mother." "Good night, Joey." "Good night. Pa." "Good night, son." There is silence. Suddenly Joey shouts, "Good night, Shane." The sound echoes through the empty room. The picture fades as the lamp dims—and the shadows restlessly gather unceasing strength....

Decisions

The astute reader will have already drawn his conclusions concerning my paranoia. I choose not to debate classification with an unseen foe; the more, especially, since—in that magnificently close-ended circle of logic required by such an enemy—debate is held tantamount to confession. Yet the modern narrative is, itself, deceitful as woman. And at this point the alternative to the charge of paranoia may be the charge of dishonesty at its highest—literary craft.

Truth, of course, if it is to be abstracted by the reader ("ruined", as the alchemist would more ambiguously say) will have no more significance than the lies of skill and indulgence I have put to my purposes—largely formless, I should say, though these may yet be. I do not write to teach (although the converse is humorously more reasonable). Indeed, if I retained half the didactic purpose of my youth, I would address myself now to the still hopeful, and end my tale with the affirmation of alternatives I never saw or understood while I was at Norfolk.

Consider what I say. I am an historian, bound by largely mysterious forces of self-explanation to the reasonably accurate rendering of actual event. Like my younger self's hero, John Webster, I do not write with a "quill winged with two feathers". And in my labors, often do I find the needful leisures of revision a burden past supporting.

It goes like this, chum: if I'm going to re-order events I couldn't handle, then why the hell can't I straighten them out while I'm at it? Dick and Karen, if once the actual names of actual people, are now my creatures, my property. A phrase, it would seem, barely whispered, should suffice: "For God's sake be nice to each other!" I am, in short, no less susceptible to the fruitless agonies of the might-have-been because I am a teller of tales. Yet fruitless they are, for—as the folk music I now loathe insists—"you reap what you sow". I cannot whisper to them, and they would not hear me if

I could.

So, the paranoia? Well—you may yet be surprised by the ending. And I would remind you of the risks involved in classifying a suspicious man's dealings with a world wherein all things change. Still, the reader may justly demand to know the following:

Shortly after they met in New Brunswick, Dick and Karen became lovers. This relationship they maintained throughout the remainder of the school year, despite the logistical difficulties which attended a week-day separation of fifty miles. He visited her each week-end, and more often during the following summer. As lovers, they were more successful than most; less, probably, than others. Their relationship developed out of what seemed to them a stunning coincidence in taste, habit, humor and philosophy. If, in actuality, this coincidence was merely the result of continual adjustment and flexibility—why, what lovers have ever been brave enough to believe this? They were not fools; yet, or hence, they did not question what they had.

When, the following autumn, he was drafted—the crisis intensified their love. Now she traveled to Fort Dix to see him each Sunday. And, when he was assigned to New York City, she continued to visit him. By way of a characteristic Army blunder, he—a former English major who could not type—was made a typist at the Induction Center on, Whitehall St. He was given a rent and food allowance (which, with his regular pay, amounted to fifty dollars a week), and left, when off-duty, to his own living arrangements. New York was congenial to him, and so long as the hours were nine to five the arrangement seemed tolerable. He rented an apartment which she visited as often as she could. And another year passed in this fashion.

Yet, inexorably, the pressures formed. As her graduation approached, the tension of too long forestalled decision narrowed their joy. A summer stretched before them like a panting woman upon whose body action must be taken or denied—a summer during which she must decide whether to go on to Graduate school, and, if so, where. He would leave the Army in the Fall, and must make a similar decision. Now the visits were tear-stained and the loving was spasmodic. The films and books and folk songs which they shared seemed now more personal, as they wandered into their decisions.

She left for Norfolk to try it out, to judge her talent and Yale. In June she visited him twice from Norfolk—a worried, tired girl unsure of her skills. In these visits she found him more tense than ever, unwilling to understand what was rapidly becoming for her a private life in music.

The Army had reduced the Whitehall St. personnel by half, and increased the work by more than triple. As New York's summer heat increased, so did his hours. He was required to work from 8:00 A.M. until the day's assignments were finished. Often he had to stay past midnight. Through July, he averaged fourteen hours a day. A few hours on Saturdays became necessary. Some Sundays, when he did not have to serve as

Charge of Quarters, he slept all twenty-four hours.

He had always hated the Army, and now he was exhausted by it. When her letters stopped, he applied for leave. It was denied. His stomach registered the first symptoms. It began to flutter inside him. For three successive days he went on sick-call; each time he was accused of malingering, and returned to work. She had given him no phone number. His letters were not returned, but neither were they answered. A strange silence had settled over Norfolk like the shadow-evil out of the North in some ancient folk-tale; and, as to a moral in such a tale, this silence seemed so inexplicable that it palled and oppressed without causing the kind of pain that can be diagnosed.

Given to melodrama though he was, it was several weeks before the flutterings of his stomach became more sinister. Then, suddenly, the silence and the awkwardness of their last meetings slammed together to release energies of suspicion or knowledge. The strain of his work had weakened him, and his flesh yielded before the impact. In one day, his eyes glazed over, the snakes in his belly broke free of their bonds, and his head began expanding. The nausea, the dizziness, the peculiar detachment did not escape the notice of his superior, who reacted fearfully and recommended two weeks leave.

But the leave hung, Army fashion, in the hundred intermediate holes of command. Before it was approved, there was time for Dick to write an ultimatum to Norfolk. Karen answered immediately by telephone and they quarreled violently. She called again, and he told her of his two weeks leave. She seemed delighted. And in this condition he came to Norfolk on a Friday evening.

And thus, through the inevitability of after-fact, I found myself sitting on the grass not far from the barn, alone on a Sunday morning, trying to write a story....

Green Green Rocky Ink

A story follows its form as surely as water takes the shape of its container. When I told Karen I was working on a story, I had been more optimistic than honest. For prose was still new to me then, a luxury release which the disciplines of poetry and the Army had driven me to. Once while making love to Karen in my father's car, I broke the little rod which connects the accelerator to the gas pump. But the car was new, and its idling speed sufficient to drive to a garage. I wrote that summer as if I expected a similar miracle. A story will take its own form, but it must be driven and steered faster than idling speed. I was, however, as cautious as I would have been with any new high-speed vehicle, and I held the handbrake firmly. By now I had perhaps a dozen separate fragments I could work on, liberate at their own speeds.

Possibly, if you are the indulgent reader I take you for—possibly, I could dazzle you now with some prose flourishes. You will have already noted that I fancy myself at times a stylist, and I do not think it beyond my competence to dazzle—providing, of course, you should choose to let me. "Cover her face;" cried Prince Ferdinand, "mine eyes dazzle." Obedient as always to such example, and, as always consistent with my larger purposes—I shall reduce the glare a trifle and tend more strictly to the business of credibility. Not that there won't be times when you might wish for more illumination: this grass business, for example, that I keep darkly hinting at. Still, all things are ultimately simple, and only their arrangement constitutes truth (I might add "their style" as well; but having just sworn to tread the humbler path, I'll leave that judgment to you).

At any rate, I was—as I've been saying—an imaginative, ambitious, but cautious young writer—quite incapable of bringing any work to the garage. I would dip a toe into the current and then, uncertain how to maintain my balance, I would do the one thing guaranteed to lose it: I would remove the toe and shake it dry.

So my notebook was filled with just slightly dampened scraps of fiction and considerably longer, though probably drier, sections of non-fiction — essays, in short. One of these essays concerned Shane.

I do not think you are quite prepared for it yet, in full, at least. There has probably been enough of that sort of thing for now. It is chiefly valuable to me as a primary source for much of what I then thought about Shane. I never throw away my notebooks. As I have suggested earlier, so much of my life now seems ghost-like, so many of my thinking verbs conclude with 'ed', accident alone could dispose of my notebooks. And no accident has befallen the text before me now — no accident, that is, save the large one, experience, that has rendered so much of that young prose as obsolete as fidelity.

It is a brown-covered notebook, creased and spotted. The cover predicts ninety leaves. But there are ragged strips of paper caught in the rings to testify, without my having to count, that at least a few leaves have been torn out. Probably they became letters to someone. It is a "Rutgers notebook". It cost forty-nine cents, and Karen bought it for me in the Rutgers book-store.

The notebook is entirely filled with writing; that is, each page contains at least a note. One happy accident most concerns us here. On the morning I have been almost describing, I picked up Karen's pen by mistake. She had, that Spring, taken to writing in green ink. (It was more a joke than an affectation. Though I'm not sure any lovers' joke can be explained, suffice it that in reference to a green blouse she often wore I had begun calling her a "green slug." (How "slug" became a term of endearment, I'll leave to your own recollections of the absurdities of love.) For this reason she had written me in green ink, and the habit stuck.) I was considerably annoyed when I realized that I had taken her pen, but I kept forgetting to exchange it. As a consequence, all my writing at Norfolk is neatly delineated by its color. I can actually date this writing, establish (roughly) its chronological order, and, in short, make sure of what I was writing (which is at least a clue to what I was thinking).

A musicologist I know slightly (and do not much like) is working on some grand project involving an intricate analysis of a Bach score. The details interest me little, except for his plan to use inks of different color to help organize his work. Isn't that a pleasant metaphor? Autobiography could proceed visually with a minimum of confusion or dishonesty. Primary source material would be in green, emendation in red, recollection in blue, plain fiction in black. Or — one could work out an elaborately symbolic system: green for youth; red for passion; black for sobriety; true-blue, perhaps. Isn't it fun? A casual glance, and you would know when to skip over a passage. Young ladies could be saved by a warning to avoid the red.

And none of this is entirely without point. The green ink of the Norfolk writing is interrupted here and there with other colors of revision. The revisions are nearly always stylistic ones, and they are nearly always improvements. There is no way for me to determine when they were added. To quote absolutely from the green would be in some cases impossible (revision has often obscured the previous writing); in all cases, it would be unfair to a boy who would never have permitted anyone to see what he regarded as an imperfect copy. As I quote, then, from my younger self, I will be quoting material that is not necessarily "first draft". But this concession I will make to history—I will not now revise what I find in the notebook before me.

The green entry begins:

> *So I had this week's leave and I decided to go see Karen who was at the Yale Summer School in Norfolk, Connecticut; my intention—to lie around for a week: grass and trees, musicians and artists—and no Army. All of which was a noble if lazy idea and I did it.*

> *But within a day I was hung on my lack of function which I lay by playing ping-pong; word spread, that is, that a stranger had appeared to take on the school and guys would come in to play me....*

On the next page appears this strikingly familiar line:

> *Norfolk, Connecticut is a fairy-tale place where Yale University used to conduct a summer-school for music and art....*

It would appear that I had some thoughts of a story about Norfolk. But, while each page continues beyond my quotation, the ink is black and represents addition rather than revision. Apparently, at this point my energies became more meditative, or, perhaps (for a story does follow its form) they simply came under control. This is what I wrote on the next page:

> *Observe—as Prince Ferdinand would say—my meditation. If there is anyone of my generation who has not been formed by movies, I have not met him yet. When I was in the Army I wrote a war-poem, narrated by a sergeant recollecting his impressions of a battle. I sent the poem to a former teacher who sharply criticized "my" clichés, "Blood was all around", "some of the boys", "a flesh wound", "getting it"—war-movie dialogue, he called it, and could not have known that I had taken these phrases directly from tales that veterans had told me.*

> *Had these veterans simply absorbed the diction Hollywood had imposed upon the war? No soldier, as Tolstoy pointed out, understands the battle while he fights it. Yet all soldiers can recall the battle in terms of over-all strategy they have since read about. The after-knowledge informs their memory, and how can we know that the diction of after-knowledge has not also informed their memory?*

> *Young lovers often indulge in the highly sexual posture which movies may have created: the boy lies with his head in the girl's lap while she strokes his hair. No one questions the pose; it*

comes with the Hollywood stamp of decency. Yet girls do not put their heads in the laps of young men; there is no film precedent.

In movies the artistic principle of audience expectation—that principle which shapes all crafted work—has been strangely perverted. All love novels do not end tragically, yet my generation expects the illicit lovers of film to come to grief and pay, if not repent. And the very metaphors of conventional cinema— the "clinch" that signifies sexual union—have through the realism of the art form become real things in themselves. No one, I'm sure, has ever mistaken sex for the "literary" pounding of the surf. Yet I am mildly astonished that there has been a generation procreated since my own—so profoundly do films influence us.

I indulge myself, of course, for the point will not be debated. No one will deny that people respond to crisis in the manner of—say—Betty Davis or Humphrey Bogart. Yet I often believe that every role we play—from the way we hold a cigarette, to the ideals we claim—is motivated by the movies which informed us.

There are songs, of course, and poems, and tales, and theater, too, I guess; nor was the world ever quite without the arts from which men learn to live. Yet cinema has made the roles easier. As a member of the most self-conscious generation ever spawned, I sometimes wonder how we ever know anything about each other....

You will readily perceive how early I had struck upon my essay style. With what regret I here deny myself the pleasure of some prose analysis. There has been so little change—even the fear of "self-indulgence", and the Prince Ferdinand tic. Delightful! (There are distinctions, of course, some agreement problems in parallel construction; and the sentence about "songs, poems, tales, and theatre" seems to scan—or, at the least, its rhythm suggests a recent writer of verse.)

What I was thinking, at any rate, seems pretty clear. And then there continues a paragraph which supports my earlier hinting that this, too, may have been a story. It further suggests that I was thinking about my thinking:

Do not lose patience with me. In the lightening manner of thought I traveled these trails for a minute as I lay there ordering the vaguenesses I not quite apprehended. And then, in the manner of thought, for perhaps half an hour I thought only generally of these things—as fully formless as the shadows I had been watching. Then the reason for my thinking was recalled to me. It did not surprise me that Karen had quoted from a movie, I had, myself, been once quite literally wrapped up in it....

I do not have to point out how easily I could have used this section, fit it into my present narrative without comment. The germ of this book has been long growing. But at this point on the page the green ink shifts into the following dialogue—more properly, I suppose, a skeleton scene mostly constructed of dialogue (I am more than a little chagrinned to note how much my ear has since decayed):

> *"What are you thinking?" she said.*
>
> *I shook my head ruefully and turned away. "Thoughts no self-respecting lover ought to be thinking."*
>
> *"Tell me anyway."*
>
> *"Well, the fact is I was thinking about Shane."*
>
> *"Shane!" She wasn't angry at all—more amused, possibly amazed.*
>
> *"I'm afraid so, I was thinking how we are responsible for what we are—like love, for instance. And it's the only way we can live. But, still, it's an evasion, because we also know how little control we have."*
>
> *"How romantic!" she said. But she said it without bitterness. In fact she was nibbling at my ear, I turned to kiss her.*
>
> *"Why Shane?" she asked.*
>
> *"Oh, it's not really very close.... Why the hell do I have to lecture all the time? It's not very close anyway."*
>
> *"I loved it, you know." she said.*
>
> *I leered at her. "What did you love? Shane?"*
>
> *"Oh that, too," she giggled. She looked away. "I really did, you know—I mean both." She sat up and drew her legs tightly together. "I don't think," she smiled demurely, "I don't think I'll tell you which I liked better."*
>
> *"Coy Karen." I sighed. And then I said, "I think maybe I love you."*
>
> *"Oh yeah? Well listen. Buster, I'm not a "maybe" girl."*
>
> *We were close, I thought—warmth, despite the pedant's nonsense. She was neither "had" nor "committed", just warm—a person I'd known for years. It wasn't even a tactic. She expected me to love her.*
>
> *"Maybe," I said, paraphrasing my uncle, "maybe I'll remove the 'maybe' when I meet you for breakfast tomorrow."*
>
> *"Oh—this time you're going to remember to ask me to see you again?"*
>
> *"I hereby ask to see you again."*
>
> *"Well...maybe." She paused. "What about Shane?*

I don't even know how it comes out, you know."

"You can guess, I expect."

"Yes. Starret comes to and shoots Shane while he's shaking Marian's hand."

"Brilliant."

"Of course. And then Joey—who is really Wilson's son by a previous marriage (having been stolen by Gypsies), only now you can see his birthmark...where was I?"

"I don't know. But you're right, because Joey...."

"Oh yes. Joey goes off with his mother who isn't his mother...."

"Yes, Leaving Starret and Riker...."

"No, really. What about Shane?"

"Do you really want me to?"

"I might as well get used to it, I guess."

"That doesn't sound like a maybe."

"It isn't. Come on. Talk."

"But it's so boring.... all right. I was thinking of the moonlight scene where Riker comes to offer Starret a job."

"That was a great scene."

"Yes. They talk and each one explains his position. And it's a toss-up because they're both right. Riker won the land from the Indians, and Starret respects that. But it's—I suppose—just a process...nomad versus town...something like that. They're both right and they keep telling each other that they're reasonable men. And they state their reasonable positions. And there's just no chance for compromise or reason, because it's not reason but process that's the point. And yet they think it's up to them. And all the while...."

"All the while," she said, "Shane and Wilson are staring at each other, and it's really all between them."

Ginny

It was now shortly after lunch-time, and my green green rocky ink was interrupted by the one major figure in my story who has yet to be formally introduced. Ginny is a good-sized girl. And in tribute to her form I'm going to come at her in a rather round-about manner:

Joe Reily is a pretty ridiculous figure. He is forty-six or so and a journeyman violist. Whenever he can get away from his wife (who "doesn't understand him") he spends the summer at Norfolk re-charging his youth by teaching and seducing young girls. He is not exactly the ass-pinching type—a dirty old man, yes, but without the grace of overt lechery. His personal and professional life is so generally confused that he can work adequately (by which I mean lecherously) within the "mixed-up" role without most people realizing the inadequacies of its actuality. Joe Reily has been defeated so many times that he wears the manner of defeat attractively. That he is quite illiterate, that he is incapable of sustaining a satisfactory relationship with any woman over thirty—facts of this sort have won for him the reputation of "a nice guy". People put it this way: "Joe's a little crazy, but he's a nice guy." This is meant to be a compliment.

To be fair (one must, of course, be fair even to moral cripples who badly need killing), I would have to say that he is in some ways a nice guy. I, too, fall often into the common delusion that incompetents are nice—when, that is, they lack the intelligence of, say, an Alvin (whose capacity for self-examination often pushes him into the category of "irritant"). Actually, Joe Reily has his moments of introspection, too. I once heard him declare that maybe he was a little confused, but, after all, it takes all kinds....

Joe wore his stupidity to advantage. Lacking the literacy required for self-analysis, Joe worked easily within his superficialities. In plain language—there are people who spend their lives acting out and mouthing clichés. They do it honestly and consistently, and no one ever believes they mean it.

But there were things about Joe Reily that were not so "nice". Seducing his students, for example. There is this damned "emotional involvement" nonsense that musicians espouse (more dramatically, I think, even than actors). And for a middle-aged teacher to trade on it seems to me not nice. The fact that "making beautiful music together" (he would say, "playing intuitively") is the most ludicrous of clichés, seems never to have bothered him much—understandably, given the extent of his perceptions.

I have heard it said that he is "warm". And this may be true. He is a hand-holder and—like all incompetents—self-deprecating. To the female, "warmth" may be just so described. Joe knew a lot of famous people, too, and this fact, no doubt, radiated some of his "warmth".

That particular summer, he was visited several times by his friend, Alex (whose wife doesn't understand him). Alex makes millions in Hollywood, composing and arranging scores for movies, and his quite ordinary music is much applauded by some people I know. It contrasts, you see, to advantage. (I should say that I am sometimes tempted in a similar aberration to give credit to journalists who avoid some of the clichés of their genre. It's true enough that I can't stand musicians, and may be writing unfairly. Yet—I ask you—how can a million-dollar enterprise be art?)

Well, Alex is every bit as nice as Joe. And the point of all this is that Joe—not for the first time—had been upset by a girl who went to bed with him readily enough out of the usual wrong reasons, but who also got out of bed and stayed out of it. It occurred to Ginny, sometime during their flesh ritual, that Joe Reily might be a warm, nice guy—but just a bit limited. She had left him for Ross (the blues guitarist), and was in the process of telling this to Joe as they were returning up the path from lunch. Alex was a bit behind them, no doubt fingering a reserve million or two, ready for a last-minute intervention.

The details, I learned later, of course, from Ginny. What I actually saw was her abrupt turn away from them. Then she walked along the path past where I was sitting. A few steps by me, she paused and turned back toward me. Then, gathering her beautiful legs together, she sat down on the grass and began talking to me. She had honey-colored hair, and was, in fact, the girl whom I had already seen at the Friday night party.

It was years later, when I was teaching at a co-ed college, that I first realized in what specific ways girls resemble flowers. The metaphor is common and works readily. Yet its actual precision may overwhelm the man who has never gone beyond the notion of delicate beauty. Girls are colorful, symmetrical and fragrant. When they are happy, they bloom, and when they are despondent, they droop and wilt.

They are fragile, though they do not as a rule close up at night. All this. But consider that all this—the blooming and stretching and spreading of breasts and arms and legs, the delicate fragrant symmetry of sex—all this is to provoke fertilization. There have been times when, puritan that I am, I have found myself, by way of this metaphor, almost regarding sex as the natural process so many books insist upon. Gazing upon a classroom of rainbow tendernesses, I sometimes comprehend Joe Reily's problem. For the budding breasts and dewy eyes and pollened limbs, the gloss of skin and hair, all these manifestations of morning-nurtured beauty—these tender petals opening for enlightenment and seed—these are the melancholy measure of passing time. They cannot all be gathered. And when I am as old as Joe Reily (not so far away, I fear), I may find more sympathy for the middle-aged lecher.

But Ginny—oh Ginny was a flower; large, but not gross...a rose, of course, sensual like a rose—with a fragrance as unsubtle and as enticing. A yellow rose, for color...for the heady heart-stopping aura within which she voluptuated—red...deep extravagantly sensual lush blood-rich red. Ah Ginny....

"I'm Ginny." she said. "You were here when I went to lunch, and you're still here. Don't you eat? You didn't miss much really. Are you George's little brother?"

Through her first dozen words I had been planning to be a dedicated writer, but her last sentence caught me. "Little?"

"Nothing personal. Younger, I mean," She smiled. "I have reason to know you're not little."

"What do you mean?" I was confused, overmanned.

"Jesus!" she said. "Don't get cute. The party...your pants, baby...before you hit your head on the bookcase."

The writer evaporated, leaving an aridly nervous boy. No...the opposite, perhaps, drenched—out of my depth. "Oh." I said. I stared at my feet. "I didn't break the glass."

She laughed. When Ginny laughed, her whole body followed a primal dance figure. "Good." she said. "That's the way when I'm like this—I just had a scene and I'm a little high...good. I was afraid you were going to come back with something about these." She gestured vaguely at her breasts. Her mouth pouted as she tucked in her chin.

"Ginny," I said, "I'm flustered, I'll admit. But those aren't the first breasts I've ever seen."

"Not bad, though...?" What is true is not necessarily coarse. Ginny could tease.

"Not bad." I said. "No, I'm not George's little brother. What made you think so?"

"You look like him. You were with Karen. I thought...."

"I'm Karen's boyfriend." The euphemism sounded rather silly, and accounted, I thought, for her puzzlement.

"I didn't know...what are you writing? Are you a writer?" And—yes, suddenly I was a writer, without much trouble telling her about my writing. Ginny was a good listener. To say that her body relaxed would be to mislead. Nothing that statuesque ever entirely stops posing...misleading again—she was not marble, and her poses were of understated motion. Yet she listened well. Her flesh became surrounding detail to center her face. Her eyes followed your words out into the air; her mouth formed upon continual agreement. Her listening pose encouraged, I even read her my dialogue.

"That's very tender." she said. "I mean, it's warm... I had a lover once who used to talk movies at the damnedest times, too. What is it? a play?"

"No...well, it's mostly, I suppose, recollection. But it's for a story, I think."

"Well, thank God you're not afraid to write it out. I had a writer once who was always blocking up because he was afraid to use anything personal...embarrassed, you know. I mean once he was working on this scene—he was a playwright, you see...you've probably heard of him... TV...Morris Wright...play-Wright, you see—" she laughed easily, "and this scene was a conversation in bed...you know, afterward...and the dialogue stunk, so I said, 'Morris, baby, just get a tape recorder and get it down.' I mean, why not? But do you know—he was afraid to. I mean, he'd scream when he came, and I thought why not work it in for character? And he said, 'for Chrissakes, Ginny, how can I ever get that through on TV?' But that wasn't it, I knew, because he'd always wanted to write a novel, too—don't you think playwrights are always a little nervous about not being serious, making too much money and all...I never knew one who didn't want to write a novel—but the real reason was: he knew if he put it in about his screaming, the other women he'd slept with would know he was talking about himself. But why not? God! It was the most exciting thing about him. It always sent me over...."

And this was the way Ginny talked, with a casual vulgarity that suited her appearance so well it never seemed inappropriate or even inelegant. Talking with Ginny, one always had the illusion of intimacy—the relaxed calm of bed-talk. I was—I'll confess it—enchanted.

"But this—" she said, pointing to the notebook, "it's so close to being cute. I mean, you take some chances here. But I think it's mostly OK— more tender than cute—and I like it."

So we were friends. And, as friends do, we assumed each other's life history without asking, and acted upon the unstated facts of mutual knowledge. But one assumption of mine was wrong. It had to do with music.

"God, no I..." she said. "I paint. I mean, I'm an artist, I have fun, too. Sometimes I write—poems, mostly."

Then she recited a short poem she had written. I cannot quote the poem, except for one line, but it was like all the poems you have ever read in women's college literary magazines—narcissistic, reeking of sensuality and masochism. She was a snowflake, as I recall it. The one line I can quote is the last: "(something something) pulsing panting and white." I told her it sounded familiar. She asked me what I meant, so I told her. She roared with laughter and slapped my knee.

"That's what Milton said...just exactly what he said—after he'd made me. Before, of course, I just oozed talent, Milton...you know...ah...what's his name...Krassel. Milton Krassel—the poet. Jesus! What a sonofabitch! He reads his own stuff to his classes at Barnard, and those dumb girls—do you know what Dorothy Parker said about Barnard?"

"If all the girls at Barnard..." I began.

"Were laid end to end..." she added.

We chorused the last line together: "I wouldn't be a bit surprised."

She continued: "That's it, anyway. Me, too—a famous poet...oh hell, I was young. I think maybe it's a little sick, though. That's why I just heaved Joe Reily. Christ, I don't need a father anymore. Not that he isn't good enough. But God!"

"I like you." she said. "I'm a lousy poet and I like you."

"Ginny," I said, "I like you. Was that Reily you were arguing with?"

"That's him—him and his friend Alex. I could tell you something about old Alex too. But it was no argument. I just said 'no more'. I suppose you think I'm promiscuous."

The question took me by surprise. It had not occurred to me to apply moral terms to her. I told her so.

"I'm sorry I asked." she said. "Maybe you will now. I get the feeling you're kind of moral. Maybe it's...was that the first time? the dialogue, I mean. You said it was real...."

"Real—hell!" I said. "Yes, it was real...it was our first date."

She stood. "As my dear friend, Milton, would say, let us pursue this multi-splendored day."

It was not from "Paradise Lost", I decided, and I also stood....

Norfolk Summer School

Having now brought you to the principles of my plot, I shall—with flamboyant self-consciousness—remind you that Jacobean plays tend to boil somewhere around act three, simmer for an act, and then lift the lid again. Since I prefer my metaphors well-done, I will avoid the obvious, "climax"; I did not, that day, do much more than boil a bit with Ginny. Yet it would be questionable taste for me to omit reminding you of the resemblances between life and the art of John Webster I was always distilling. I am not quite anxious to draw any exact correspondence between common steam and the mist of the Duchess of Malfi. But the insanity of the play is not more unreal than a caricature of the world. And if Bosola calls life "a general mist of error", and claims that the deaths attending Act V are mistakes made "in a mist; I know not"—I feel no great reluctance in further cooking his metaphor. I am, after all, engaged in an exercise of historical interest, not in the business of telling life as I now think it. (If, by now, you think that you can compass me and know my drifts, I had better remind you that he also says the accidents are like those seen in a play. Fair warning?)

What obsessed me about the Duchess had much to do with a hundred years of critical error. Webster had written, as I thought, a tragic farce or, perhaps, a stylized dance of death. But good gracious! the noble Duchess dies in the middle of the play. What kind of tragedy has a meaningless and bloody fifth act—devoid of the tragic heroine? My answer, then: John Webster's tragedy. The consequences—God help us all—the consequence of undirected passion is the "hideous storm of terror" which is death in the mist.

So, you see, I'd have to say that art isn't life, except occasionally; but if you heap a few passions raw into a pressure-cooker and generate a little steam—why, the mixture you produce is less disorganized, but considerably more confused than the original was.

In short, you have had two and two-thirds acts now, and I don't intend to digest the rest for you. I couldn't, if I wanted to. It adheres to me as well as to itself. But I'll condense. I doubt that I have the stomach to recreate entirely the simmering. That's the horror, isn't it? When the valve blows I'll be amenable to detail again. In a room full of steam, details create no difficulty in selection.

Now for some local color:

Norfolk is in the mountains of northern Connecticut, near the New York and Massachusetts line. The summer-school in Norfolk is a former country estate. It covers much ground. It contains woods and fields, rocks and streams and paths. It touches the town—which is small and characteristically New England—at every unexpected turn of a path. Roads appear just over a ledge or behind a formal garden. There are buildings with practice rooms and cottages for the professors. There is an auditorium for concerts. The students board in private houses in the town which is always near.

The school divides nearly evenly between musicians and artists. It is titled, The Summer School of Music and Art, and the ordering is correct. Emphasis is on the musicians, who practise, study, rehearse and attend classes most of fourteen hours each day. The work is exacting and arduous. The musicians are serious students who are struggling, fighting, perhaps, to improve and perfect their skills. They are led, tutored, and relentlessly driven by brilliant professionals. Over the summer weeks, fatigue invests these teachers with more of the inspirational than of the instructive. Their example is, at the same time, a heavy, nearly insupportable frustration.

Each of these young students has seeded years of labor. Often they have been unnatural years—cut from normal childhood society. In this one, a family's recreation has been staked; another has been nurtured at the cost of friends. All have sacrificed much of their lives in this blind hopeful planting. For they practised when the other kids played baseball, and they gave recitals while the Proms went by. They all have talent, hope, doubt. Many of them have turned in toward their work; they warm in its seclusion. They know little else but music. Some have turned upon it, protesting its unnaturalness. These brave, venture, and try to understand. And there are those of hardier stock who have done neither—who have lived in the harrowing, not much changed, understanding little of it.

Yet for even these the pressure in this ten-week time grows oppressive. This summer-school is the first harvesting. The unmarked packets, from which was sown such diversity, will produce some tentative labels here. One common label is "mediocrity"; it will appear often.

So they work—these serious young people. They attend classes and rehearsals throughout the day. There are hours saved for practice. At night there is studying to be done for the next day's classes. Sundays, when there are no concerts, are free. But the students meet and rehearse among themselves; for there is not time enough through the week for their group projects.

So it goes through ten weeks. Each week accumulates more work to be held over for the next week. The school bases its work-program on the self-discipline of students who have years behind them of the habit. It maintains its program by group example. The students compete with, and so encourage, each other.

By mid-course, however, the word "discipline" loses its original meaning. The musicians are caught in a run of work which only accelerates. There is no longer free time in which to choose "duty". Week-end parties, which began the term as outlets, become frenzied tense affairs. Toward the end, musicians drink to sleep. Personalities become confused; relationships are deformed. A broken string, a spilled ashtray—these become issues of profound importance. Some students quit; there are break-downs; there are attempted suicides.

And then there are the artists. It would be unfair to describe their ten weeks as only play. They have their projects, their classes, their work. But they are very different people. And to anyone watching their careless ease outdoors, swiping at a colorful canvas or studying it with a leisure cigarette—their time seems fun.

They are testing and proving, but there is no result to be objectively appraised. They, too, hope and doubt; but this summer will answer neither. If anyone marks their canvases with an "A" or an "F", what will it mean?

They have chosen a work which has transcended their society, but has not isolated them from it. Most of them understand their artist's need for living. Each creation reflects experience; they have been taught this and many understand it. They are slightly mad, perhaps; they are expected to be. They have accepted a life which people think of as slightly mad. They paint and study and play and paint. A canvas may take a minute or ten weeks.

It is impossible to walk the estate without stumbling upon an artist. A visitor will be hailed, pressed for an opinion—more often than not, he will be sketched. The artists are everywhere, within and around the musicians. The town closes them together....

Complications?

And so, with some ease, Ginny escorted me around the estate. She knew everyone, of course: Ken, who paints landscapes that look like Walt Disney illustrations and talks while he paints about the "super-perception of the child-mind"; Pam, who splits the wood end of her brushes and inserts a cardboard handle into the crack ("she says she wants it to flutter," said Ginny, "but then she's never been laid"); Archy, who plays the trumpet when he is not doing cross-word puzzles ("he told me he got soured on the whole thing back in grade-school when he played "Frere Jacque" for the school assembly, but he forgot to clear the spit valve and everybody laughed at the gurgling. He says he has to admit it was the dampest "Frere Jacque" they'd ever heard"); Mark, who works on one huge canvas which had been growing progressively darker through the weeks and is now entirely black; Julie, who plays the cello, who never says more than "hello" till she is drunk("at which time her language is something else"); Frank and Tom, whose friendship livened the gossip of the middle weeks, but has now cooled considerably ("I was there when they broke up. Jesus! Talk about divorce! I thought they'd start fighting over who got the children"); Rick, the comic-book reading violinist ("I mean, really illiterate. He was a child prodigy and he never learned to read").

We strolled for nearly two hours while Ginny sketched character and introduced me to the darker side of Norfolk. The introduction was not formal. To most we merely waved.

"Why, Ginny?" I said.

"It's the tightness." she said. "We live together...there's Bob...over there. He tried to kill Ross, one party, with a fork. Ross is a pretty uncomplicated guy, I mean, he's calm...like George. And Bob's his best friend...I don't know why. But Bob—he plays bass...he used to play jazz somewhere—Bob got high and wanted this girl who was all over Ross. She—you'll meet her; she's hard to miss...she's Alicia...isn't that pretentious? —she plays, I think it's viola. Anyway, she'd come to the party with Bob, and there she was with her hands in Ross's pants...I mean, I thought it was a bit much...so Bob picked up this fork and went for him...."

"And...?"

"George stopped him. He gave Alicia hell, too. They've stayed OK now for a while. It wasn't Ross's fault. He's OK. In fact, I've been going with him."

"Euphemisms, Ginny?"

She laughed and led me over to speak to Bob. He was staring morosely at a broken-off bass string in his hands. He held it like a garrote.

"Hi, Bob." Ginny said, "Where's the tramp?"

Bob was not amused, "I'm looking at her." he said. "Ross must be out of his mind."

I introduced myself.

"Met you at George's party," he said. "You here for long?"

"I don't know." I said.

"Well, watch your ass with this one." Then he grinned. "You're here to see Karen, I hear."

"Yes."

"She's OK. Everybody likes Karen." He looked back at Ginny, "Hear you dumped Reily. He was crying a while ago. Didn't he know about Ross?"

"None of your business, pal." said Ginny, as we wandered off.

"George is over behind the shed." Bob called after us.

We walked for a while. Ginny was silent.

"No more dirt?" I said,

"Bob's evil." she said, "He loves to start things, I mean. Like that...he was bugging about George...."

"I saw him cheat at croquet yesterday." I said. "The other guy wanted to kill him."

"Somebody will." she said. "I wish they would, Jesus! that fork business! He's tried suicide a few times, tried, that is. He's looking to get killed, but he can't do it himself.... He almost raped me once...."

"God!" I said.

"Oh, come on, baby...it happens."

"You said 'almost'."

"Yeah...I slugged him and ran...it was easier for me—I had a skirt on; he had to get his pants back on before he could follow me. Men are OK,

I mean, and I love them...but I'm not a thing. He grabbed me again later, and Jesus, I was pitiful...so I almost thought 'what the hell'...but he got so excited he spoiled it, I guess. Maybe it's as good. I'm not a man. I don't know...."

I was as titillated as you are now—more abashed, perhaps. But I did not mutter short non-committal incoherencies all the while we strolled. The walk was not entirely Ginny's monologue. I vaguely defended Bob by explaining the murderous passion aroused in me by certain Army types. Then, to show I was civilized, I told an Army story, suggesting by hand gesture and lip curl that all could be endured with humor: "...so since this guy answered 'that's not it' to everything from orders to officers to equipment, finally there's an inspection coming and they panic because they don't want the General to see some nut wandering around saying 'that's not it'. And they go up to the guy and they say 'the General's coming here for an inspection.' 'That's not it' he says. 'Yes, we know,' they say, 'we want you to take a little rest in the hospital during the inspection.' And they put him in the psycho-ward. The Shrinks come in and try out everything on him. They give him a word-association test and he looks at it and says 'that's not it.' They give him a Rorschach and he says 'that's not it.' And—I'll condense—everything they do he just says 'that's not it.' So finally they decide he's incurable and it's better to get him out of the Army than throw away money trying to cure him. So they write up a discharge for him and they call him in and give it to him. 'That's it.' he says."

I am fond of such humor, being temperamentally attracted to shaggy-dog philosophy. But George, it developed, had been a conscientious objector, and I smelled disaster in that direction. So I began the appropriate Cummings poem which Ginny, of course, knew well enough to join in on the funny lines.

We were some distance down the rocky dirt road behind the barn, when I realized that Bob's information had been wrong. We had not seen George.

"I know." said Ginny. "He meant behind the other side."

"The one with the trees?"

"Yes. He likes to paint there. Everybody goes the other way—by the road."

"I sort of wanted to see him." I lied.

"So did I—till that bastard broadcast it to all of Norfolk." She meant Bob.

"Are you in love with George?"

She moved to face me. She had large blue honey-hair type eyes. "What's love?" she said.

I burst into laughter; she, into tears. She was a girl, after all. And if—Crashaw-like—I saw smooth non-engagement diamonds chip from her eyes for a moment, it was for only a moment. I put my arms around her immediately and she soaked the front of my neck. Then she wrenched loose as if I had grabbed her, took several steps off the road, and sank, shaking, onto a grass and pine-needle carpet—leaving me in the ludicrous uncertainty of the male role. I followed her and sat beside her. Again I put my arm around her. And the flood turned off.

We sat, silently watching the small stream that curled below us. It is one of the pleasures of Norfolk—this cold clear brook.

Where we sat is, perhaps, the most pleasant observation post.

The dirt road from the barn inclines downward for several hundred yards, before it nearly levels with the stream and curves to avoid it. The stream flows parallel, to the left of the road, separated from it by a wooded bank of ever decreasing width and height. The right side of the road is deep thick forest, but the bank side is slashed with natural drains. The melting snow, in one place, has carved a slope, the width of a road, which descends steeply from the gravel, then levels after ten feet to a rock ledge, an arm's length above the stream. On this slope a number of rocks have been abandoned by numberless thaws. But the process has been so gradual, so gentle, that the rocks have reached some accommodation with the grass and fallen pine-needles. The grass is luxurious, and the needles were still soft as we sat upon them, watching the stream.

I had disengaged my arm as soon as the shaking had stopped. It was my left arm, and it still ached from two nights before.

"Shit." said Ginny, after a while.

"What?" I was a little abstracted.

"I said 'shit'. You had every right to laugh. But it wasn't as dumb as you thought."

"Oh." I had found my role. "It wasn't as dumb as I thought."

She laughed and threw some needles at me. "I want him. He turns me on. I want to go to bed with him."

"It wasn't so bad." I said. "A while ago I almost asked you what 'real' means. Does he know?"

"Everybody knows."

"Well, well. Poor Ginny. Did you ever lose before?"

She grinned, "No. It's a little frustrating. Did you read The Sun Also Rises? You know how Brett bawls on...what's his name...the eunuch's shoulder and says, 'Darling, I've been so miserable'...? It's frustrating... goddamn frustrating."

"His name is Jake, and I'm not a eunuch!"

Ginny stretched out her long legs before her and leaned back on the heels of her hands. Her face was in no way spoiled—softer, perhaps. The tears had harmed no more than had the winter snow.

"Do I have to remind you that I know?" she said.

Now I was looking downstream toward the footbridge at the curve of the road. It is a wooden rustic sort of thing, another pleasant feature of the view from where we sat. You can see the bridge and the town it leads to, but the bridge cannot see you.

"Do you want me, Dick?" said Ginny.

I shook out a cigarette and lit it. "Isn't it pretty to think so?" I said.

"When you held me..." she paused. "I felt that you did.... I don't know if you knew it...."

"Look—you're very attractive, and I know I look like George...."

"That's right." she said. "But it's Karen, isn't it?"

"Of course it's Karen. What the hell do you think...!"

"You've never slept with anyone but Karen...? since you've been going together, I mean."

"No."

"Why not?"

"It wasn't worth it—the complications...."

"What if she was—I suppose you'd call it—unfaithful?"

"It depends, I guess. Things happen...they aren't necessarily serious... they wouldn't have to matter. Look...I...."

Ginny shook her head. "It's not just George." she said. "Jesus! I mean, I'd be out of my mind if I was that confused. But...hell, you do think I'm promiscuous."

"Ginny," I said, "I'm mad because I'm tempted; because I just said 'it wasn't worth it' instead of 'it isn't worth it'; because Karen and I have been a little tense lately; and you turn me on; and I think if I tried...wait...." I held up my hand, a traffic signal on a snow-formed road. Something sardonic had formed near the corner of her mouth. "...I don't mean you're promiscuous, and I don't mean I'm moral, and I'm not judging, and...this is a speech...how does it end?"

"Sex is too beautiful to waste?" she suggested.

"Don't tease me," I said. "I'm too easy. I only mean...."

"You judge." she said. She nodded. "You judge. But maybe not me." She softened her voice and, sitting up, touched my hand. "Here's some ego for you: I really did want you. And I think you're dumb. But let's be friends. OK?"

It was OK....

Ping-Pong Perhaps

Ross joined us for supper, Ginny sneaked me some food, and we talked pleasantly long after the meal. They invited me for some beer and I agreed with pleasure. Ross wanted to pick up his wallet which he had left in his painting clothes. I protested that, since they had provided the meal, dessert was up to me. But Ross insisted. As the discussion became tedious, Ginny jumped up, declaring she would get the wallet while we argued. She ran lightly ahead of us toward the barn. We followed more slowly. I liked Ross. There was a little of George in him, I thought—his carelessness, anyway.

"She's hoping to see George." said Ross.

It had been a rough day, but now, a man-of-the-world, I merely nodded.

"She try you?" he said.

What, exactly constitutes chivalry? I was a man-of-the-world, so I said, "Yes."

Ross laughed. "I like you." he said. "Karen said I would, and I do. What do you think of Ginny?"

"Zenobia." I said. "Nice...like a sister to me. Can she paint?"

"She could...I don't know now. Come see."

He led me to the room off the ping-pong room. "These are George's." he said, pointing to the paintings hung around the room.

I examined them and disliked them. Ross, assuming I was a tongue-stopped layman (which I am), did not press me for an opinion, but led me into the ping-pong room and up the stairs to the barn-like studio.

It is a large room—a loft, slant-roofed and plain board sided. The floor and walls are paint stained, colorful, messy. Twenty-five or so painting areas are defined by easels, benches, or nailed up canvases. They clutter the loft, but increase the impression of vast and cold space. The canvases shriek "student" and "talent" with equal vividness. There were no landscapes, but at the far end we saw George and Ginny. She was holding Ross's wallet in one hand, gesturing with the other at a canvas which was evidently her's. It looked a lot like George's. There was nothing awkward in their pose. They had seen us and were not troubled by the concomitant fact.

"Where's Karen?" said George.

"At some damned concert." I said. "She's transportation."

"Oh." he said. "I was just cleaning some brushes, I thought perhaps we might play a game."

"Do you play ping-pong?" Ginny asked me. "Jesus, of course...Karen's so good...that's why. Well maybe we can postpone the beer."

"No, go ahead," I said. "I'll join you later."

"I'd kind of like to see this." said Ross, "I hear you're good."

"Aw —" I said, "audiences humble me."

We were near the supply and sink shelf, and I poked at a blob of half-dried paint. It yielded, but did not split. George was nearly done. While I played with the paint I watched him put away the brushes. It is always tempting to sentimentalize an artist; but there was in his hands a compromised conflict of precision and delicacy that I found interesting. Women's obsession with male hands has always seemed unsubtle to me. And clichés about craftsmen seem woman derived. Yet Karen was right in calling them "artist's hands". I deliberately refused to see whether Ginny was watching. I put down the paint-ball and took out a cigarette. I looked about the room for the "no smoking" sign and, finding it, told them I would go down stairs for a smoke. Ross offered to warm me up and hurried after, followed by Ginny. George was washing his hands.

Ross and I volleyed for a while. He played not badly at all. Still, it was no contest, and he seemed relieved to give up the paddle to George. Ross drank from the water fountain while I stubbed out my cigarette. George and I exchanged pleasantries and began volleying, while Ross went over to one of the couches opposite the side of the table and sat with Ginny to watch the game.

I am not humbled by audiences. They often excite me to excellence. As there is comedy in the head-pivoting of a tennis spectator—so is there a ludicrous pendulum suggestion in the eye motion of the table-tennis watcher. In an especially dull or even game, it often seems as if marionette wires connect ball and head; for the head—ever so much more subtly than for tennis—does turn. It is, I sometimes think, hypnosis gone wrong, by some daemon master mesmerist perverted—or, occasionally, a centering on some basic primal rhythm: Tic...Clop; Clip...Took. "For every action there is...."

I see this from the corner of my eye, and wonder why the head-shake is the expression of the negative. I see this—for I am listening for the ball; I am connecting my own pulse to my (presumably) equal and opposite opponent. I play by ear while watching ball, foe, and fan; the clock above the water fountain, the green green table, and the top of the net. I am playing well—not perfectly—but with a form suggestive at least of what perfection I am capable. The lighting is harsh and the green table surface has patches of water-glaze, like the even sparkle mirage of a sun-slanted dip on a tarred road as you approach it fast. I swoop gracefully to back-hand, and the heads move with me—unconscious sympathy for the hours of practice (my backhand has not always been this thing of beauty), I look back up across the ceiling and light and then square ahead, ready for the return—and am giddy. And the heads to my right still turn with the exchanges. I receive the ball and arc it high—spinning as imperceptibly rapid as the earth must seem from star-distance. And the heads go with it, and back, turning, shaking as if in some universal perplexity. Qualified negative and the "I don't know" of bewilderment fuse in a metaphor of indecision which is the visual counter to my own steady-rhythmed, if inconsistently paced, pulse.

George played very well.

Suddenly Ginny jumped, "Oh Christ!" she said. "Here comes Reily. Let's get out of here."

George and I looked at each other and shrugged like twins. "Oh well...." We were reluctant, but we left.

Casey's, George's Place, Bed

Casey's was packed. People and beer spilled indiscriminately from booths and tables. We joined a group around a large table in the center and drank. There was little opportunity for speech. The noise oppressed, and I found myself out of cigarettes. I walked to the back of the room, then through the doorway into the bar where the townies drink. The bar was not especially crowded, but the path to the cigarette machine was awkwardly routed. I had not the correct change. I moved to the bar, and was ignored by the bartender for some minutes. I stood there coughing, a dollar bill in my handkerchief. Then my palm was crossed with some silver, and the dollar extracted from the other hand in one fluid gesture. I turned with thanks. The bartender had not yet even glanced in my direction. I might, conceivably, have eventually coughed up blood. I got my cigarettes and returned to our table in the other room. I stood leaning over to whisper to George. I had to shout in his ear.

"Come over to the doorway. I think I've found Alvin's visitor."

"Wilson?" said George, smiling.

I nodded, "Drinking with the men."

Ginny and Ross looked up, but George calmed them with a wink. He followed me to the doorway and together we looked in at my benefactor.

He was quite alone—isolated by an empty stool on either side—sitting hunched over and facing the bar mirror. His Levi's were dark brown and his zipped motorcycle jacket was black. He was not seven feet tall, but he was taller than George.

A dark nerve was ruffled; he turned slightly and saw us looking at him. His hair was long and black, and his moustache drooped slightly at the corners of his mouth. I could not resist a wave, which I hoped suggested gratitude. He pivoted easily on the bar-stool, swinging his long legs around to face us, exposing black engineer's boots. He raised his shot-glass in a half toast to us, and then organized the most subtle double-take I have ever seen: only his eyes shifted, more in intensity (dilation or its opposite) than in direction.

So we looked at him and he returned our stare. We were smiling and so was he. It was, I thought, an unreasonable impasse, George did not offer to enter the room and our stranger did not leave his seat; he seemed almost to invite us in. I responded with logic and the limitless absurdity of which I am capable. I raised my cigarette pack aloft and pointed to it, miming grotesquely the offer of a cigarette. He understood me and shook his head slowly, then placed his shot-glass back on the bar and, turning toward us again, removed a pack of Camels from his vest slash pocket and removed one deliberately. I nodded. His eyes did not leave us for a moment. He reached his right arm back across the bar, sliding his shot-glass out of the way with the back of his hand, scooping up a pack of matches in the same motion. He lit his cigarette and continued to look at us, I shrugged stupidly, pointed to the bartender, and shook my head. George had not yet moved. I put my hand on his shoulder and motioned toward our room. He nodded and we left.

"What do you make of him?" I asked.

George faced me, dead-pan, "He's no cow-puncher." He drawled.

Then he moved over to whisper an invitation to Ginny and Ross to join us for a drink at his place. They agreed, subtly extricated themselves, and we left together.

The four of us had a quiet drink in George's living room. It was not yet late, but I had the sense that Ginny and Ross might want to be alone. I was surprised, then, when Ginny requested a song. Ross seemed not reluctant to play, and performed both "Young Woman Blues" and "Cocaine". He played very well. I was about to make a request of my own, when Ross handed the guitar to me.

"Karen tells me you play." he said.

I was modest, all too aware of the adoration which had informed Ginny's listening during the past few minutes. "Jack Elliott stuff." I muttered. "Changes in genre...." My hands continued, suggesting that perhaps this was not the time.

"Really?" Ross was eager. "I dig Jack Elliott."

I twitched at the strings a bit, un-tuning, tuning again. They were not musicians anyway. I sang a couple of "country" tear-jerkers, cracking my voice appropriately, thickening my accent, diverting attention from my inelegant play. My audience was amused and entertained. Emboldened, I stood, slung the guitar rock&roll style, and sang "The Wreck of the Old 97" (which chronicles, as the title suggests, the railroad tragedy of a brave engineer trying to maintain schedule:

They was comin' down the grade, doin' ninety miles an hour,

When the whistle broke into a scream;

He was found in the wreck with his hand on the throttle,

He was scalded to death by the steam....

and concludes, obscurely, with a verse that has no apparent relevance to the rest of the song:

Now all you ladies take heed of my warnin'

From this day on and learn:

Never speak harshly to your true lovin' husband —

He may leave you and never return.)

I finished, then pushed the guitar behind me and assumed a lecture position.

"Now I want to say," I mimicked, "that what I really dig about this song is the last verse. I mean, can you see all these ladies who have been speaking harsh words to their husbands—can you see them standing around, waiting for their men who are never returning? I mean, just watching and waiting. These are the true artists—right?"

It was successful. Everyone laughed with humor. And no one laughed too much. And no one said "touché". I timed the pause accurately and sang the one Van Ronk song I can play. It is a "nonsense" song called "I Buyed Me a Little Dog". It begins:

I buyed me a little dog,

His color it was brown.

I taught him to whistle,

To sing, and dance, and run.

His legs, they were fourteen yards long,

His ears, they were broad;

Around the world in half a day

On him I could ride.

Sing Tarraday —

sing Tarraday....

There are many versions of the song, and each has charmed me. It continues, recording the purchase of several more wondrous and impossible things. But the way Dave Van Ronk sings it transforms the nonsense into tragedy. Somewhere between the rasping voice and the tender silly words the song becomes a sad chronicle of growing up—the passing of childhood illusions, and the seeking after more mature, yet no less illusory, dreams. I cannot rasp like Dave Van Ronk, yet my arrangement partakes of the same melancholy, and my husk produces a kind of tension. I sang and played it well, and put over to an attentive and saddened audience my favorite verse—the last:

> And he who tells a bigger tale
>
> Will have to tell a lie.
>
> Sing Tarraday—
>
> Sing Tarraday.

The smiles were not jolly (nor do I think the verse is essentially funny). There was silence for a while. Then Ginny asked me how I had begun playing.

Shortly after we had become close, Karen and I discovered a mutual interest in folk music. This interest preceded the "boom", though not by much. And with the "boom", Karen began itching for a guitar. I put fifty dollars hard earned TV repair money into a guitar for her—a birthday present. The week of her birthday she bought herself a fifteen-dollar guitar. The timing so infuriated me that I said nothing, bought her a record (or something), and kept the guitar myself. I practised secretly, observing and profiting from her own practice.

When I could vaguely play a few songs, I finally performed for her and told her the sad story of my purchase. She bought a better guitar for herself, and we learned the rest together—she, the musician, of course, always weeks ahead of me, patiently enduring my outrageously sulky clumsiness. By now we played rather well together.

It was a funny story, and it cheered my audience.

"She is good." said George.

"Yes." said Ross.

And we all murmured praise, subdued, as if for a relative who has passed away. During the next pause Karen's absence became more and more obvious, and Ginny and Ross began a leaving shuffle.

"You should sing one before we go." Ginny said to George.

"After the parody?" he laughed. "Oh well—it's my only song, Ross...?"

So Ross played it, and George sang,

> I'm an educated man
>
> To get more sense within my head I plan....

We applauded and Ginny and Ross stood up to leave. George took the guitar back to its case in the dining room. Ginny hesitated, I stood up. She came to me and kissed me lightly, "Come swimming with me tomorrow." she said.

"Yes," Ross chimed in, "I'll be in the photo-lab all day."

"All right," I said, "I don't have a suit...."

"Meet me on the road." she said, "Get a suit from George." Then she called, "Night, George."

He and I saw them to the door, and then returned to our seats, feeling a little like some travesty of marriage.

"Coffee?" said George, after a silence.

"Maybe a cup," I said, "Let's drink it in the kitchen." The kitchen was more appropriate, and we had several cups. We talked long and easily—about books, mostly. There was no mention of absent people, nor of any Norfolk gossip. It was book and movie and music and art talk, and I enjoyed it. I cannot imagine anyone failing to enjoy such talk with George. He is a graceful conversationalist; his voice moves over awkwardness as a snake over a stick.

Conrad—a mutual love—began and ended the talk, George had never read The Secret Agent. I was moved to read him my favorite passage—the stabbing of Verloc, with the shock-like suspension of actual time. It reminded George of Youth. He found the scene he meant, and reminded me of it. This moved me to tell George my theory of the fault of most modern writing: how, unlike Conrad, the writers who have learned from him use psychology to explain behavior, instead of as a metaphor of behavior. George was interested. He had had some such feeling, himself, but had not yet quite articulated it. He wondered if the way men thought of their behavior was not more important than its actual causes. He was so close to my own reasoning that I grew quite excited. The point was exactly that, I told him; rationa1ization and what informs it—books, movies, music—these were what mattered, not the actual reason. He agreed.

We had a good time—the kind of time I had not had since the days of JD and Pete. We spoke of Marlowe as if he were a friend in California. Even The Secret Sharer was recollected, placed between our cups, and dismissed without implication. Finally I reluctantly yawned and said goodnight.

"Breakfast...?" said George.

"Maybe." I said. "Doubtful...."

He nodded, and I went upstairs. I watched the shadows for a while, but was soon drowsy. By the time Karen returned, I was asleep and did not hear her.

Sometime during the night I set up straight saying, "a yo-yo."

Karen answered sleepily, "What?"

"A yo-yo." I said. I was wide awake.

"It's just a bad dream, honey." she said, not moving enough to shake the blanket which muffled her voice.

"No," I said. "That's it—if someone watched a yo-yo contest his head would move up and down like a nod. Yo-yo means "yes"...because it's an even sillier sport and it begins with "Y". But ping-pong begins...."

I couldn't figure it out further, I lay back and was soon asleep again....

Water is Erotic

I slept late the next morning (Monday—if you are keeping score). It was sunlight that roused me finally. It had moved gently and unobtrusively around the house to stream finally in through the gaily colored curtains above the bed. I had slept well, and I greeted the sun with affection; it seemed a good omen.

I half expected to wake George for coffee, and was blearily part way down the hall when I recollected Karen. I returned to our room, not very surprised to find the bed empty. I probably would not have left it, had she been there, I thought. I had also some dim notion that her absence was, for some reason that I ought to know, the proper condition of the day. I stood in the room for some time prodding my brain, absently rubbing my left arm—still sore from three nights ago. Then I saw the note on the table by the bed:

> *Sorry—tried to wake you—car again—tonight.*
>
> *Love, Slug*

It was written in pencil and looked vaguely foreign. Ah—I had it: the pen.

Having satisfactorily returned the universe to order, I strolled downstairs to find a message on the kitchen table:

> *Bacon eggs milk in refrigerator. Bathing suit on table. Help yourself,*
>
> *George*

So, musing on Marlowe's musing on Kurtz's "telegraphic style", I breakfasted alone, feeling quite thought-after and irresponsible. I was in such high spirits, I even hummed to myself as I left the house. It was the part of "Young Women Blues" that goes:

By my side he left a note

sayin' 'I'm sorry, gal you got my goat.

No time to marry

No time to settle down....'

Realizing what I was humming, I stopped, clouded over, lit and coughed on a cigarette. The sun was gentle—no day for that kind of nonsense. I deliberately hummed the song, and strolled to the barn, where I spent a couple of hours genially slaughtering a few people at ping-pong.

One of them, the son of the current gardener, even told me I should play George sometime.

"Oh?" I said, "Is he good?"

"No slam." said the boy seriously. "But he won the regional championships a few years ago."

The information cut through my humor and startled me. "What regionals?" I said.

"Eastern Regionals. No slam, but you can't get anything past him. Real steady."

"Did you see him?" I asked.

"Sure, Dozens of times."

"No, I mean in the tournament."

"No, the guy from Hartford told me."

"What guy from Hartford?"

"Snyder, I think...came down to play George last year. He's the champion."

"Of Hartford?"

"Yeah, George took all seven...said if George would of turned pro he could live off it."

We had finished playing and I was leaning against the water fountain. For balance, I asked, "What makes you think I could beat him?"

The boy laughed, "Don't think you can. Nobody here has. But think you got a better slam than the Hartford guy. Be fun to watch anyway. Thought you might be a brother or something. Ginny told me you wasn't. Don't play like him anyway. Johnsons, for instance, play like each other...."

I might have explained to him the confusions attending some telegraphic styles, had I not been reminded of Ginny and my promise. I walked slowly down the road, troubled perhaps by something other than Ginny or style or the surprising news about George's fame.

She was sitting on the grass and needles, reading a book, when I reached her.

"Didn't think you were coming." she said.

"Hasn't anyone here heard of the first person singular pronoun?" I said.

"What?"

"Nothing. What are you reading?"

"Poems." she said. "You talked about Webster, so I dug out this anthology. He's here. See? 'Call for the robin-red-breast and the wren'."

"He's a playwright." I said, "Taking those songs out of context is like talking without pronouns."

She squinted to see if I were serious. "Why didn't you tell me he's in 'The Wasteland'?" she said. "Here: 'But keep the wolf far thence....' I never knew that was Webster. Why didn't you tell me?"

"Because I'm sick of Eliot and people who quote him when I mention modern poetry."

I sat down. "I'm kidding," I said. "I have a destructive sense of humor. I don't mean you. You've slept with more modern poets than I've read."

"Destructive—shit!" she said. "I thought we were friends, darling. I'm not so hot for you I have to take that!"

"No." I apologized. "I mean...look, did you know George was Eastern Regional Champion?"

"Of what?"

"Table tennis."

"No, I know he beat a guy from Hartford last year. Somebody told me."

"He never told you?"

"No. Is that good? Eastern Regional?"

"Yes, it's good. Very good."

"Well, you're not so bad, seems to me. You stayed right with him. Do you know what I always think of when I see a ping-pong game?"

I got up to a squatting position and scooped a handful of needles, which I sifted methodically.

"I won a tournament once." I said. I nearly told her the details, but stopped, feeling inexplicably reluctant. This was not the only confusion in my head. I was certain I had not mentioned John Webster to her. But the sorting was tedious and required articulation.

"I mean," I went on, "I won a big tournament once—lots of small ones, of course. But not the Regionals."

I opened my hand and shook out the few large ones remaining. "Look," I said, "when we were playing last night, was he slamming at all?"

"George doesn't slam. Karen says...Ross says sometimes you don't even think he's there. When I watch a game, it reminds me...."

"But last night...?" I repeated.

"No, it was hard and all, but he wasn't slamming. He can't slam, every-body says. Why?"

I sat down again and moved close to her. "It's funny," I said, "I never noticed. And now I can't remember."

Ginny took my hand and mocked wide-eyed head-shaking consolation at me: "It's no shame to lose to a Regionals champion. Don't cry, now. If George is better, you can only learn from him."

It didn't amuse, but the hand contact quickened. "Where do we swim?" I said. I gestured at the brook, "There?"

"Toby." she said. "It's a little lake."

"How do we get there?"

"Hitch-hike, don't worry, I'm popular."

She pulled me to my feet and we returned toward the main road.

"Just for the record," I said, "I never said anything about John Web-ster."

"No?" She was all innocence. "Must have been somebody else."

Ginny was popular and we had a ride within minutes.

Toby is a pretty little lake less than five miles outside Norfolk. It has a pleasant beach of fine sand. Off the beach, about twenty yards out, is a small float for diving. And there are the usual picnic tables and shacks for changing. On this beach on any given afternoon through the summer can be found one-third of the school. The water is muddy but cool. Sun warms the beach early in the day, and the water is relief—even in the clear air of the mountains of Connecticut. The temperature drops sharply at night. But, insulated and benevolent, the waters of Toby are often warm after dark, perfect for the nude swimming which is very much a Norfolk sport. At sundown, a heavy chain is drawn across the rough dirt road to the beach. Then, those who will must park their cars and stumble through the dark to reach the pond. The nude swimmers have been interrupted a hun-dred times by every level of officialdom—-from the F.B.I, to the school's Directors. But in no instance were the flash-light raiders anything more, after all, than sadistic friends. This sadism, too, is a Norfolk sport.

Across the pond, perhaps half a mile distant, are a few well scattered private cottages. One of them was the bearing point that Ginny insisted we make for.

"Insisted" is the kind of distortion I must permit myself in recollection.

It is not always easy to be tolerant of one's younger self. And, God knows, if he were truly I, if time and experience had not irrevocably separated us—I would find it impossible to forgive him much. Yet, like a father who has been through it all himself, I can smile occasionally and say "yes, son, I understand."

Ginny in a bathing suit—white, in two brief pieces—was a flower I had never seen before. Her honey hair hung free, blending about her shoulders; for the sun had melted her skin an even smooth, rich gold. This was the color of her. The texture seemed as perfect. The fine silk hairs of her legs and thighs lightened at the tips, enticing as velvet, as irresistible as moist oil paint. Her legs were long and finely formed. From beneath a skirt they flashed the kind of promise so often unfulfilled; yet now, from the tight line of her bathing suit they yielded the rare beauty of bare perfection. Ginny's hips were large, perhaps, for even classical proportion. Yet the fault (if it could be so called) excited all the more. The suit—a modified bikini-cut—clung beneath the extreme of the curve. She knew... she understood the value of imperfection.

Her breasts—must honest recollection prove conventional? Her body was exciting; her face, beautiful. The fragrance of her beauty layered the heart and throat of those who saw her. She bloomed and softly glistened in the sun. And the live muscles beneath her alchemy-confounding skin rippled like the fragile petals of a breeze-ruffled flower, A Rose! Oh yes, I mix the colors, I know; but the collective truth of her was—a Rose.

I stood before her in the too-large hanging suit I had borrowed from George, and reverted to the religion of my most primitive ancestors. The tasty rumor had been whispered round that she was "Tanned all over". How perversely unsophisticated pure carnality can be. Even standing still, her body arched and twisted, and there was no whiter skin in the creases of her flesh. Yes—she was tanned all over.

And I—the color of a New York office and a one-room apartment—in one intuitive moment of internal sensitivity, I felt my muscles sag; sinews soft as maggots, flesh rippling like custard pie.

When Ginny suggested that we swim across the lake, my brain responded sensibly; but my manhood.... Oh yes, I understand and sympathize: Ginny's suggestion was insistence.

I am a fair swimmer, but I knew my chances of drowning were better than even. I had been riding subway cars for much too long. Sheer stag ego moved me across the lake in a cumbersome side-stroke that, I too late realized, was as flabby as my body looked on shore. I rested on my back from time to time while Ginny hovered near, bubbling like a golden fountain.

She was not deceived. She was, perhaps, even concerned. She joked at my pride, but made the joke, encouragement. And finally I felt weeds twitching about my legs, and stood nearly knee deep in muck. I breathed heavily, my hands on my hips. Form required that I swim the last few yards and, eventually, I did, Ginny beside me, praising (with at least some seriousness) my heroism.

We stood on the shore, looking up at the cottage porch a few feet ahead.

"Come on up." she said, taking my hand as if to support me. "I know where there are towels."

She led me up the wooden stairway. She walked lightly to avoid the splinters. I was too exhausted to care, and I slumped when we reached the porch.

"Poor darling," she said, "You just rest up."

She walked over to a small locker near the screen door, and took out two white bath-towels. She tossed one to me. Then she knelt down and felt inside the locker.

"Aha..." she said, "I thought so."

She returned to sit beside me. In her hand was a pack of cigarettes and a book of matches.

"Wonderful!" I exclaimed, seizing them. "How did you know?"

"I've been here before." she said. "It's Reily's place. This is where he takes his daughters. Moonlight on the lake... ah...shit! I don't regret much—but that.... The bastard's got the door locked, and I can't get at the bathrobes."

I was surprised she had come here now, and I asked her about it. She exhaled smoke from the cigarette I had offered her and returned the cigarette to me.

"He won't be here." she said. "He's off with your beloved."

"Oh? I didn't know."

"Dear old Joe...old, anyway. Yes, didn't she tell you? He's coaching her quartet."

"No, I thought she was transportation again."

"Sort of, I guess, though more driver than transportation. It's George's car, after all. They had to go to New Haven to pick up some music. Joe's car is getting greased or something. Maybe it's Joe that's getting greased—I can't remember."

I leaned back against the railing, looking out over the lake. My leg muscles had hardened and felt almost buoyant. Where there had been exhaustion was now a warm tingling. My skin was pleasantly taut. I flexed my muscles.

"I wasn't sure I could make it." I said.

She laughed, "I wasn't sure either. But you did. My hero!"

She reached for the cigarette, and I returned it to her. "God! water is sexy." she said, stretching out her legs. Then she stood up. "To hell with the bastard's bathrobe." she said. "I've got mud and sand in my suit and

I'm damned if I'll itch any longer."

"Well," I said, "I can go down on the beach while you dry off."

She smiled. "You couldn't move five yards." she said, and got up herself and walked down the stairs carrying her towel.

I smoked another cigarette. She had disappeared from my sight and I leaned back to relax my neck.

"Hey," she called after a while, "I'm dry and decent. Come talk to me."

I stood and rubbed my calf muscles. I walked slowly down to the beach. It is a narrow strip of sand that blends into grass near the corner formed by the porch stairway. I turned the corner and saw a dry and very decent, but entirely uncovered flower in the crannied wall.

You see roses all your life. You are told and know that they are beautiful. But "perception", says Alfred North Whitehead, "is simply the cognition of prehensive unification". Mussolini's son-in-law dropped bombs on Ethiopians and called the explosions "roses". Juliet Capulet liberated them from nominalism. Burns personified; Hugh MacDiarmid nationalized; Blake spiritualized; Hawthorne.... Oh look not long, young man, into the center of the rose. Perhaps if I could explain how far removed from "the war of the red and the white" my thinking really is; perhaps if I could now sort out the color-texture-fragrance confusion of my meaning; perhaps if I dared risk pornography—I could tell you what God and Man is. Will you believe the delicacy of her pose? For I'll not go beyond mine. Shadows blossom even in broad daylight.

"Hi." she said. "The sun feels wonderful." I sat beside her and was silent.

The return swim was no less arduous. A strong late-afternoon breeze had come upon the lake, chopping water into my nose and throat. It took me more than an hour, gurgling, floating, dog-paddling; but I made it and stretched gratefully at last upon the hot sand of the beach. I closed my eyes immediately and slept for nearly an hour.

When I came to the sun had all but vanished and the lake was calm again. I sat up and looked about me. The shore was deserted except for half a dozen people at the other end of the beach. I stretched, and began brushing sand from my legs and chest.

"Here. We don't want our hero catching cold."

It was Ginny. She had changed in the bathhouse and was handing me my clothes. I brushed myself some more, and began dressing over the bathing suit which had dried on me while I slept. Ginny lit a cigarette for me and sat down.

Water is erotic. The fatigue of swimming is unlike any other; it functions like alcohol, I think—warming to a casual laziness. I looked at Ginny and smiled. I looked at the fragile bathing suit which rested beside her. She had given me a head start in our swim back, time for her to put on her suit again. She had caught up with me easily, of course; but I had been preoccupied with self-preservation and had not really seen her then or when I had collapsed on the beach. To see her now, demurely bloused and skirted, was a startling change in perspective, I wondered briefly at my memory.

She easily guessed my thinking and, I am sure, enjoyed it. To know visually but not tactually the body of a lovely girl is a pleasantly unsettling experience. My knowledge delighted me; that fact delighted her.

"Uh...." I began.

"Yes...?" she laughed encouragement.

"Uh...I guess we missed supper."

"Yes."

"The lake seems calmer now."

"Yes."

"Maybe it's not calmer. Maybe it only seems calmer."

"Yes, maybe."

"Are you annoyed with me?"

"Don't be silly."

"You're not quite right about morality, you know. I'm not especially moral. That's not why...I'm just very conscious...." I almost stopped, hung on the word, "of complications and the way...what they do to people."

"I know." she said. She stood up. "Come on—forget it. I'm not insulted. I know you...I enjoyed being wanted. I mean, my ego's Ok. Your's should be in pretty good shape, too."

I stood up and took her hand. "How do we get back?"

"We walk." she said. "Out to the road, anyway. Someone'll be along."

We walked the path from the beach out toward the road. When we were in the trees out of sight of the beach, Ginny stopped suddenly.

"Hey," she said, "you did like me, didn't you?"

I turned around to face her. "A rose." I said. "Have you ever read Hawthorne?"

She wrinkled her mouth. "Scarlet Letter?"

"No...well, yes, there's a rose in that, too. No, I mean Zenobia... Blithedale...she's a rose." I frowned. "I'm sorry. It's the way I am. I can't help making associations like that."

She shook her head in wonder, her hair rippling over her shoulders, gilding the white of her blouse, forming about her breasts.

"Scarlet Letter...." She still shook her head. "You do think I'm promiscuous."

My arms lifted, bent and inarticulate. "No." I said. "It's Zenobia—and she's wonderful...like you...but it's a lousy idea."

Ginny took my two hands and stared into my face. "I'm all covered up." she said. "It can't hurt, and I'll do it."

And she kissed me (just like that) long and firm and soft.

It's the P.T.A

Ken, the Disney artist, gave us a ride to town. He dropped us off at Casey's, where we ate a hamburger apiece. We were nearly finished when Alvin joined us for a cup of coffee.

"Well well," I said, wiping some ketchup from my lips, "what's the latest on the mysterious Wilson?"

Alvin chirped a little. "He won the swimming meet today—that's what's the latest."

Ginny and I exchanged guilty glances. "There was a swimming meet?" I said.

"Yes." He cocked his head like a proud mother. "You should have been there. He won by twenty yards. Nobody was close even."

"Oh." I said. I stared into my coffee.

"That's something, huh? Too bad George wasn't in it. Everybody figured George would win."

"He didn't swim?" Ginny's voice was casual.

Alvin started fumbling for change. He methodically checked each of ten pockets, then returned to the first, and found his money.

"Huh?" he said. "No. He was working or something. Too bad. Would have made it a better race. I've seen him. He's good. I'd still bet on Wilson, though. That is, if I were going to bet...which I wouldn't. I mean, I don't gamble.... How much tip should I leave? It's fifteen percent, I know, but that's only a penny, and she doesn't like me much anyway...."

"Tip? for what?" I said. "It wasn't any trouble for her. She had to come anyway for us."

"Yes...well, I don't know." Alvin stared at the change in his hand, "Do you have two nickels?" he said. "If I leave a dime, she'll think I'm coming on."

I handed him a nickel, "It's on me." I said.

He looked grateful. "I'll pay you back first chance I get.... I hear you're a wonderful ping-pong player. Would you care to play me a game?" He stood up, wincing as his toe rapped the edge of the booth. "I'm not very good...." His voice trailed away as he looked at the two of us. Delayed perception overtook his eyes.

"Of course," Ginny and I nearly chorused.

"Who told you I was good?" I said quickly.

"George." he said. "Are you sure...?"

"Sure." I said. And we walked up to the barn.

The game was a nightmare. Alvin played as he did everything else. Finally, during one lunge, he lost his grip on the paddle and nearly decapitated me.

"Maybe I should take over for a while." said Ginny.

I smiled at her gratefully.

"Well," said Alvin, "I think I've had enough. I seem to be pressing."

"Yes," I said, "I've been noticing that."

"You think that's what's wrong with my game?"

"Well," I said, "there's no doubt that you push yourself."

I walked over to drink from the fountain. Alvin hurriedly pushed the button for me, shooting water into my face.

"Gee—I'm sorry." he said. "I'm awfully sorry." He dragged a handkerchief out of his pocket. "Here—it's clean...honest...."

Ginny started laughing. I followed. Finally Alvin joined us. "Definitely beer time." said Ginny.

"Definitely." I said. "Alvin, you haven't seen Karen, have you?"

"No," he said. He looked at us. "Or...Ross." he grinned.

I slapped him on the back. "Good for you, Alvin." I said. "Well—will you join our clandestine orgy? as a chaperone, of course."

But he had a test to prepare for, and begged to be excused. Ginny and I returned to Casey's.

The test seemed a wide-spread curse and there were few students in Casey's. Those who were there were mostly artists who nodded to Ginny and discretely left us alone. We drank several beers, very much enjoying the gossip we were stirring. We laughed over Alvin's playing.

"You know," said Ginny, "when I see a ping-pong game I always think of the cartoons we used to have at the Saturday afternoon movies—where it would be a song, I mean, and they'd put the words on the screen, and a little white ball would bounce on the right word, and everybody would sing along. I used to like those cartoons."

"I always thought they were pretty dull." I said. "But boys, you know...." I started laughing. "That's a wonderful idea. I mean, about the ball. But think how the words would come out if Alvin were playing."

"Yes." she laughed.

I asked her if she had heard the details of Wilson's arrival. She had not, so I told her. I made it good, with a few embellishments from Shane thrown in. She laughed throughout.

"Is it really true? Did it happen?"

"Collective truth." I said.

"What's that?"

"Collective truth is...well, it's like another way of saying something... metaphoric truth—the way it should have happened. Like the last verse of the song I sang; 'And he who tells a bigger tale will have to tell a lie.'"

"I see."

"For example—you're a rose."

Ginny actually blushed. I ordered more beer.

"I liked that song." she said. "And the others. You sing very well."

"It means a lot to me." I said. "I think perhaps that's why I stopped writing poems. It's hard to improve on...for example, that song George sings.... Do you know the Stan Freberg skit about Yankee Doodle, where he has the fife player in the Spirit of 76 as a jazzman? No? Well, he won't play because the first drummer plays too square—'mouldy fig', he calls it—so they say to him: 'do you want the war to end on a note of triumph or disaster?' And he says, 'Like either way, man, just so it swings.'"

Ginny raised her glass to me. "I think you're an artist." she said. "George might have said that, you know. I mean...."

I changed the subject, "Speaking of songs, there's one that Ross sings— 'green green rocky road'...."

"Yes, it's beautiful."

"Yes it is. Only, does it have verses? It's evocative, the chorus. But I was wondering what the verses are."

"Evocative, huh? I thought it was pretty."

I faked a punch at her right ear, "Come on," I said, "you're the poet, let me be the pedant. Ok?"

"The poet and the pedant...." She mused the phrase to a title, putting in the quotation marks with her fingers. "Yes...it might sell—but is it art?"

"Karen...." I started.

"You're mixing your metaphors, baby."

In all the action of the undeclared war thus far, she was here closest to aggression. I raised my hands—a surrender gesture. I was tired, of course—the swimming, the ping-pong, the beer—tired enough for confusion, for metaphor mixing.

Ginny was a courtly conqueror, or a shrewd girl. She argued the waitress into another order. Then she excused herself for a moment. When she came back she said, "I'll tell you my favorite verse. It's the second one. You aren't the only one who listens to these songs, you know."

Then she leaned forward and sang it to me. Her voice was... a lovely voice, low and sweet. I kept my eyes open while she sang:

> See that crow up in the sky.
>
> He don't walk, well, he just fly;
>
> He don't walk an' he don't run—
>
> Keeps a-flappin' to the sun.
>
>
> green green rocky road
>
> promenade in green....

"That's nice." I conceded. "As nice as I'd hoped...a poem...." I was moved, so I put on my imitation of JD: "A moral and a lesson for us all." I propounded, italicizing the words as they dropped. "Consider the crow. Let us then take lesson from nature. Consider the humble crow...."

I was fortunately interrupted by the jukebox, which now began whining a remarkably dissimilar parable about a surfer who went too far out, rode too big a wave, and drowned. We listened, hoping very much that his body might be later found—his stiff wet hand still clutching her high school ring. Ginny affected mourning, and wilted. Her hair fell across the table and was soaked in beer. It broke her method pose hilariously. She shook her hair back and sucked appreciatively at the wet strands.

"Beer shampoo." she exclaimed. She was a little drunk.

The surfing song had died mercifully, and the room was quiet again. There was subdued laughter from another booth—the perpetrator of the song—but then only quiet talk again.

"What time is it?" I said.

"She'll find us." said Ginny. "Your turn, now. Recite. Recite...your own...something you wrote before bad bad green green folk music took away your muse."

"Ok, you asked for it," I recited:

> Long hair staining the bar table
>
> Bored eyes examining a drink

A deep down dirty rhythm jukebox fable
Gothic and crabbed as you think
It is for your co-ed time the last night
Your very own all, all your very own
A Twentieth century initiation rite
And their's too and yours alone.
Exchange of old drink for new
Faithfully mirrored by the bar table
A drunken head shake and you
Rise to further twist the truth of fable:
Twist and contort
A sad sport.
And I sitting in savage judgment
I who may power you as I will
I stub a cigarette with little content
And sing to you whom I've never met
How I can make you seem
How impelling my skill
To ravish your dream
For I will tell you a secret:
I know the pulse-beat at your throat and more
I know how it will...how it will seem—
Blooded General of the Crabgrass War
Laundry tactician. Arbiter supreme,

Sweeping hair-cuttings from a kitchen table,
Sighing sympathy for a child's toothache,
Mother—wife—neighbor, sated and stable—
Memory will turn (or your heart break)
To a reconstruction of this night's mood;
Boredom to excitement, twist to writhe.
Yes, you did cheat the curfew with a lithe
Gamboling naked (or rather, nude)
On the dew-cool grass by the Sacred Path,
You charmed the moon (the night was not black);

Balm scented your pores as your breath.
Your silky thighs viced many a lover's back.

Men sang of you as I now sing,
Adored, desired with respect
Flesh, brain, soul, sense of humor—everything.
Bardic guitars praised as you passed to sleep,
Smiling the satisfactions you had wrecked.

And if I thought much on this I might weep.
For here sit I, my seer's eyes moistening,
Sobered by vision that I twist to verse,
Rather than tell you what I know:
That when my fable has become your curse—
Then, in the terrible days to follow—
Wishing will make it...almost so.

Ginny was impressed. She had, I suppose, expected comedy. In the manner of the tongue-stopped layman, she finally managed: "When did you write that?"

"This Spring, on the eve of Karen's graduation." I said. "No— it's not Karen. I don't mean that. There's this bar near Douglass—in New Brunswick—it's called Mosco's. And there's a kind of tradition...the seniors get smashed the night before graduation—it's called Senior Night. And I was watching them. I got sad for them because it was so unlike what they'd hoped...well, the poem, I hope, says it."

"Yes," said Ginny, "it does." She was staring past me into a future of her own.

It is always a risky thing—confronting the female with future, any future. I had not meant Ginny, of course, nor did the poem at all apply. Yet— oh yet—how the crabgrass terrifies. I was in command again, the integrity of my forces intact. But I had, perhaps, overshot my intention, and I was beginning to regret both the action and the fact.

"The Sacred Path—" I said, hoping to focus her eyes again, "It's a path...."

"Yes." she said. "All girl's colleges have them."

Her role was now becoming, I thought, dishonest.

"Come off it, Ginny." I said.

"Ok." she smiled. "I liked it, you know...."

Smoke from the ashtray intervened. I waved at it and then crushed out the still-burning butt.

"I didn't write it all then of course." I said. "Just maybe half. I did some work on it later.... You see, I was a little sad anyway because it was a bad mix up. I'd tried to get off work to come down for the night. But they put me on CQ—that's Charge of Quarters—and I told Karen I couldn't make it. But then a buddy of mine took the duty for me, and I came down late. But no Karen. Because, you see, she'd thought I couldn't make it. So there I was in Mosco's feeling pretty sentimental, myself...."

"You couldn't find her?"

"Oh, well...there's a happy ending. She came in later with JD—that's a friend of mine at Rutgers. She'd been feeling pretty low, too, so he took her to a movie.... He's the one who first introduced us...." I laughed. "And, you know, friends and all that—but the look on his face—I think he thought I was going to hit him or something. But I was very happy to see them...."

Ginny rested her head back against the booth. Then she raised her glass and drained it.

"Bung-o." she said. "I feel rather set up. I feel hell's own set up." She held the empty glass toward me. "Buy a chap a drink." she said.

I laughed softly. "No, Brett," I said, "I think its bed-time."

She declined the gambit, but rose to leave with me. It was very dark outside. We walked up the street toward where Ginny lived, staggering a trifle. She hummed a tune which I did not recognize. Possibly, I thought, it was from a Saturday afternoon cartoon.

"Who's Zenobia?" she said. "I think...I know, the scarlet letter is A...A for "arbiter supreme." She had some difficulty pronouncing it.

Her house was not far, and soon it was awkwardness time again. Then a car turned the corner and stopped beside us, "Well well..." said a low sweet voice, "I see you've met Ginny."

"Christ." I said. "It's the P.T.A."

Karen laughed loudly. "I'm the P.T.A., am I? Ok. Get in. Rover boy."

We said good-night to Ginny and drove back to George's.

It is his car that Karen drove that summer, for he nearly always preferred walking. He usually kept the car behind his house on a dirt driveway that dropped steeply from the top of the road leading up and around to the back of the barn. But Karen never drove that winding way voluntarily. She usually parked in front of Casey's, and did so this night. George was used to this, apparently, for he greeted us at the front door.

"You found him, huh." he laughed. "Well, bring him in and put him to bed."

I was actually drunker than I had realized, and I disgraced myself by stumbling on the divot which I had previously failed to replace.

"Don't look so guilty, baby. It's Ok. I don't mind. I think it's very nice that you've found something...to...occupy your...mind, one might call it. An idle brain, I think you told me once, is the devil's playground."

We were in our room, Karen seated in a chair which I had last seen in the dining room, I on the bed. I took off my shoes and flung them lazily at the duffel bag in the corner.

"For that matter," I said, "it's a long way to New Haven, I guess, longer than I...."

"New York." said Karen. "He had business, in New York afterward. He was kind enough to buy me dinner there."

"And just how kind were you?"

"Hey—he's just a nice guy...and, look—I'm serious. I don't mind if you.... Ginny's nice, I know. She's a friend...." Her voice became heavily underlined. "I know she wouldn't do anything behind my back. In front of me, yes, but behind me...."

"We just had a few beers." I said.

"And a walk, and supper, and a swim. I have good spies."

"I made it across the lake and back." I said. "Karen, sometime can't we...."

"In your condition? That's good, baby. Reily's towels, I suppose?"

"Yes. How do you know? Have you been there?"

"Oh, yes," she smiled, "lots of times. Nude swimming, you know."

"For Christ's sake, Karen, he's old enough to be...."

"My father. Yes, my square darling, I know. But, well—you never know do you-—these older men...nope, you never know."

"No." I said. "You don't."

"I imagine you got lots of writing done."

"Yes."

"Really?" Her voice became real again, "Is it good? Can I see it?"

"I love you, Karen." I said. "Maybe."

"Well listen Buster...."

We laughed. She came to the bed, stooped over and kissed me. She sat beside me.

"Really," she said, "don't be silly. If you want to have something with Ginny...I don't mind...not so long as it doesn't change things."

"But it would." I said. "And I don't."

"Well," said Karen, "you're free, you know."

"There are things better than freedom." I mumbled sententiously.

"Yes," she said, "to be a slave and sing praises."

Jesus. 'My wonderful beautiful existential baby'. Who could turn me with a phrase! Who knew...who understood...so much. I did love her, you know.

And then I was very sleepy. I undressed and got under the covers. My body felt warm and relaxed—muscles not so soft, after all, just relaxed.

"Let's make love in the water some time," I said. "We always used to talk about doing it...."

Karen kissed me, smoothed the covers over me, and shared a cigarette.

"Ok, I'd like that." She kissed me again. "I have a test." she said. "I'll be up late studying. You just sleep, and don't worry. I'm going to go down now and get some coffee."

She started for the door. "Wait." I said sleepily.

"Yes?" she looked back at me.

"I missed you." I said. "It was a very nice sun-set."

She smiled. "I know. I saw it on the turnpike."

Asleep or awake, my essay style is part of me; "I mention it," I said, "because the sun also rises."

Pure hokum, of course. And I do not solicit belief. But I might have said it, considering the flappin' crow that was obsessing me. And—at any rate—it makes for a pleasant transition. That was the last sunset Norfolk was to see for several days.

Reily Says It All

New England weather is, as everyone knows, capricious.

Yet it is not altogether unpredictable. "Open and shet", for example, is the "sign of a wet". And the North-east wind—even so far inland as Norfolk—is likely to be at least a "three-day blow". A soft, steady rain may fall for weeks and, if it does, mid-August is the most likely time. But with a prolonged rain comes cold—wet, skin-softening cold, that gets reluctant furnaces to working, that blankets the country in gloom. The thunderstorm terrifies. The week's rain chills and palls.

I spent most of Tuesday in the house, reading, writing, playing solitaire. Karen was not stayed from her appointed rounds. She was a busy girl now, for the academic work was building fast. She left, returned, and studied. I helped her when I could, quizzing questions and making coffee—even venturing forth for cigarettes.

Wednesday passed in much the same manner. I had toyed with the idea of climbing Haystack Mountain, which is—for what it is worth—the highest mountain in Connecticut. But the rain discouraged me. I did get out for some brief ping-pong. I even managed to catch Karen for a game between rehearsals. But the pressure on her was beginning to tighten. Her quartet had one week left before performance. The performance was important to her, and our game was not relaxing for either of us.

Thursday noon the rain slackened. We ate lunch on the wet grass outside the dining hall. Ginny and Ross joined us, and invited me for a swim. There was some joking, I remember, about having to leave the P.T.A. behind, which Ross seemed to enjoy as much as the rest of us. Evidently Ginny had told him the story. George waved to us as he passed. He, too, was busy now. For the past two days we had seen him briefly, checking the radiators, cleaning the kitchen—more a land-lord than a companion.

Ginny, Ross and I hitched out to Toby, where we found few others on the beach. The rain had only paused and there had been no rise in temperature. The sun was still missing. And a breeze came stiff and hurting across the lake. The water was black, oily, uninviting.

But we were determined. No one talked of swimming. Yet we stayed there, huddled together, drinking some wine that Ross had thoughtfully brought to warm us.

Our neighbors on the beach were an odd collection of undesirables: several local hoods, Benny the pompous art director, and his good friend, Joe Reily. Alex was not present, but his spirit hovered near.

"He plays French Horn." Ginny said. "Or used to before he started composing for Hollywood. He still does, a little. He was down for a visit the first week, and took me out for dinner. We were necking in his car. I mean, Jesus! It's ninety feet long. And there was...you know, no reason to get in the back—the front seat is big as a bed. And we were necking, like I said, and suddenly he grabbed his mouth which I'd apparently hit, and started screaming about his embouchure! Jesus, it was funny! Can you imagine? His embouchure! Then!"

I thought it was pretty funny, too, and was surprised to see Ross scowling. I had grown so used to Ginny's style and Ross's calm that it was with some detached wonder that it occurred to me that "going with" Ginny might pile pressure even for an educated man like Ross. But I glanced to our right and saw the more proper cause: Joe Reily had decided to join us.

"Well, here you all are—birds of a feather, eh?" (Yes, Joe, flapping crows all.) "Yes, well, it's too cold for swimming, at least for an old man as me." (Yes, it's too cold for an old man as you) "I hear you're in the Army. I don't believe in it myself, personally, but if it's what you like—I mean, there's rooms for all, isn't there? Anyway, what I came over to ask was about Karen. Wonderful girl, Karen—warm, you know what I mean? I suppose you'll be marrying her one of these fine days. Well, that's all right," (thank you) "but she's gotta keep playing. She's got a God-given Talent, you know. Never knew anyone who could take so many beats on one bow. God-given, that's all. She'll be a Big Violist one fine day." (if she ever grows up) "Well this cold may be a blessing in disguise—keep her practising—off the beach. Yes, she's gotta keep playing. Don't get me wrong. Marriage is a wonderful Institution. It didn't work out too good for me, but that's no reason to throw out the soup, too—like they say. Some of my best friends are married. Ha, Ha. You know, an elderly Colored Gentleman once said to me: 'it's not the dog in the fight, it's the fight in the dog.' If there's one thing I haven't learned in Life's journey, it's that Education don't mean Common Sense. I always chat with the janitors at the school, like I was one of them. I mean, they got a special kind of Wisdom, if you pretend like you don't have real good intelligence. You know what an Elderly Jewish man once told me? He said: 'a woman'—I hope this don't embarrass you—'should be entered reverently as a temple.' Isn't that beautiful? It's poetry, almost." (almost) "Not your kind of poetry—that modern stuff, T.S. Eliot and all. Oh I'm old-fashioned, I guess. You artists—I can't make head nor tail. I mean, throwing some paint on a canvas just isn't my idea. To each his own, of course. I don't know much about art, but let me tell you this: I do know what I like. But I crossed over my bridges, I guess. I was talking about marriage. Take Karen, now..." (thank you) "she's a wonderful girl, and sexy—I guess you know. But there's more to marriage than sex. It's sharing. That's what it is. It's like a good quartet are—intuitive. Take my friend Alex." (no, thank you) "He's as warm a guy as I could know, and so lonely now. His wife doesn't understand him, you see. But it's not the sex. He just needs a woman so bad. I mean, it's written all over him. It's being that there's no one to share with, you see. That's hard on a Musician," (on his embouchure, too) "more than most. A Musician feels things—like music, for instance. But, you know, he's the warmest of the guys I know—and a Creative Artist. Did you all see that movie—Slave Girl of Rome? He wrote that music. See what I mean? I mean, you can't help loving someone who can create like that, can you? Between you and me, I think Karen has it. She'll be Big someday. She's Creative. You can't teach that, you know. It's gotta be born in them. I'm a little crazy, I guess, but I feel that--in here. I mean, I don't suppose you kids believe in God, but when you've been around as long as I have you'll see that there's a pattern to things and some people have them. I know lots of folks think I'm crazy, but sometimes I just like to get away from it all—far from the maddening crowds—get out in the country and see Nature. There's a pattern, all right. I even don't mind the rain when I can appreciate the Beauties of Nature."

"You're all heart, Joe."

"Well, I'm warm. You know why? I believe in acting sincere. I mean, if you can't do anything good, you can at least be sincere about it. I always figured if I was going to have been a garbage collector, I'll be the most sincere garbage collector around. Sounds funny to you, huh? Well, you're young and the sky's the limit. You haven't known the real disappointments on the road of Life yet. But if sincerity's all you've gotten, then so be it. Spontaneous, too. If you ask me, there's too many affectations in this World of Today. I'm always spontaneous. It isn't easy, neither. Don't let nobody kid you on those. People are always ready to cut you up for it. But virtue is its own reward, I say. Be spontaneous and sincere." (what if you want to kill?) "Keep her playing. She's got a GODGIVEN Talent. Don't forget, now. She's gotta play. If music be the food of love, lay on, MacDuff—like the Bard of Avis says...."

Get the point? Ginny and I stripped down to our suits and braved the waters. Ross took out a book and read it. Joe Reily returned to his friends.

We sat on the float, but the water was warmer than the air. We returned to the water, huddling behind the float, shivering, hanging on to the wooden ladder.

"Ginny," I chattered, "how could you?"

She shook her head. Then she giggled, "Lust, I guess. He's not bad, you know. If you put a bag over his head...."

We splashed around some more. Our bodies became warmer but mine did not stop shaking. The towels piled near Ross's book drew me toward the shore. I dried myself, then went to the bath-house and changed. I joined Ross, and we managed to avoid conversation for several minutes. Ginny still splashed alone, indestructible and lovely, near the float. I put on the sweater I had wisely brought. Ross put down his book.

"He has two kids," he said. "They're both about twenty."

"Yes," I said, "they would be."

"I suppose Karen's the project now."

"Yes, it looks that way. He'll need luck."

"Yes, she's a bright girl."

"A girl, though...." I said.

We lapsed into silence.

Ginny waved gaily to us from the float. It began to rain. I felt some spatterings on my head and, without a word, Ross and I moved back under the trees. The wind increased and the lake began to simmer, its smooth rolling surface now pitted and black. Ginny was soon with us again. She draped herself in towels and sat with us beneath the trees. The other group had scattered with the rain. We were alone, three fools watching the sky close down upon us.

"There's a sign" I said, "on one of the subways. It says: 'Chicken-Little was right!'"

"Yeah—" said Ross, "all these years, putting down Chicken-Little...."

"Yeah—" said Ginny, "just dig the Beauties of Nature out there."

The wind had not perceptibly increased, but now the lake was boiling as if some agent had been loosed at the bottom.

I thought perhaps a quotation from Lear was in order and tried, but could not quite get it straight.

"We have company." said Ross.

It was Bob and—at last—Alicia, followed at a respectful distance by Alvin.

"This is really D Day." said Ginny.

Alicia was miserable—that much was obvious. Her sixty-three inch bosom may have generated some body warmth, but it was also additional surface area to be soaked by the now driving rain. She took one look at the lake and returned quickly to the car. Bob paused to favor us for a moment.

"Well well, a double-header in the rain. Ginny, you're more woman than I thought."

Ross looked at him. "Beat it. Bob."

"I'm only kidding, Ross."

"I know. Beat it."

"I thought we were friends, Ross."

"We were."

Bob stared hard at me, accusation consolidating in his throat muscles. He thought better of it, turned and walked back to his car.

Now it was Alvin's turn. He had hung back while we conversed with Bob. Now he joined us, wet and worried.

"They've been fighting." he said. "I mean, I heard them on the path. I'm not with them. Have you seen Wilson?"

We had not.

"He asked me to bring the car, to pick him up. But I don't know.... He's funny...but you don't think he'd be out there now, swimming, I mean?"

We did not think so.

But he was. Alvin had scarcely spoken when we saw a head appear at the other end of the float. Wilson had crossed the lake from the other side, his route, a direct line with the float. We looked at him. He pulled himself up on the float and motioned to us...to Alvin. He pointed his arm back in the direction from which he had come, turned and dived again. He was re-crossing the lake.

"He wants you to pick him up at Reily's." I said.

"Yes." said Alvin.

"Jesus." said Ginny.

The lake was now evenly white and black. We were impressed. We watched him till he passed from our vision and was absorbed by the storm.

Alvin sprang up and shook himself like a bathing pigeon. "I'd better get over there." he said.

"No hurry." said Ross. "It'll be a while, even for him."

"Yes, well...." Alvin turned and walked into a tree. He very nearly apologized.

Ginny said, "How long is he staying, Alvin?"

"I didn't ask." he said.

"I'm sure you didn't." I said. "But have you any idea?"

Alvin scratched his head. "Well...." he said. He reached into his pocket, produced the ghost of the handkerchief he had lent me, and blew his nose. Mucous smeared his hands and mouth—not very attractively.

"Sand..." I said, "use the sand."

Alvin wiped his mouth, then knelt down and rubbed his hands in the sand. Then he walked to the lake and rinsed. The project took some time since with every wave he leaped back. By the time he returned to us, his shoes were soaked anyway by the rain. He stood before us, flapping his wet hands helplessly. I gave him his handkerchief.

"It's clean." I said. "Honest."

Alvin was near tears, but no one had laughed.

"Sit down and have some wine." said Ross.

Alvin sat and took the bottle. It was empty. Ginny gave Ross a look one usually reserves for drunks.

And at this juncture of time and space, Joe Reily appeared out of the gloom with Karen at his side.

"Look who I found." he said.

"If it isn't the P.T.A." said Ginny.

We rode in silence back to Norfolk. Karen made one effort at conversation:

"We should have followed Alvin over to Joe's place. Joe has a bookcase I want you to see—you know that one by the fireplace—it's a lot like the one your father made."

"Oh?" I said. "Of course my father's a good deal younger."

Karen gave me a look one usually reserves for alcoholics....

Connected for a Moment

Now lately there has been some talk of fathers. Lest the reader mistake the historian for the psychological writer, let me now state unequivocally some first principles:

1. I believe in responsibility, though not—as I have already suggested—in free will—except when it is more convenient.

2. I despise the convenience of motivation-by-trauma explanations and all the other lazy paraphernalia of Freudian sorcery. I do not—like Nabokov—reject it; I simply despise it.

3. I get along quite well with my father. His only relevance to this tale may lie in these two separate incidents:

Once he told me of his surprise while seeing a movie in New York City. "They actually applauded at the end." he said. "The only time we ever clapped in a movie back home was when the reel broke."

The other incident concerns my awakening to the fact of "role-playing" when I was eight. My father had been away for several months, getting a job in another town. On this particular day I had gone fishing. I was a bookish child, and it was my first fishing in several years. I actually caught a small trout and was returning home with it when I saw his car coming toward me. I was delighted, not because I had a trophy to show him, but because I was for once a "typical all-American boy". What is more, I understood my delight and its reasons.

The more specific relevance of all this may be that I remember telling both incidents to Ginny. But that was later, when I was sick—the second time, that is....

Later that evening I listened to the orchestra rehearsal for a while. At the break I smoked a cigarette with Karen. Then I walked up the hill to the barn. It was still raining hard. I went into the Men's room in the basement and dried my face and hands with paper towels. I went upstairs and into the exhibition room, where I strolled around, examining George's paintings. They were not bad at all, maybe even good.

I heard the clop of a ping-pong ball in the other room. I went into the room. Frank (the gay) was having a bad game with Archy the trumpet player. I asked Archy if the rehearsal was over. He told me the string players were being held for an extra rehearsal. I watched the game for a while, then went upstairs to the loft.

Several artists were standing around Mark's huge black canvas. The canvas was slashed in several places. From the discussion I learned that Mark had done it himself, and had left school that day. Talk was also that he had belted Benny before he left. It seemed a private sort of gossip, and I went back downstairs. I challenged the winner and sat down to wait. Ginny came down from the loft and sat beside me.

"Did he really punch Benny?" I asked.

"Yes." she said. "George will get the blame, of course. It's bad."

We watched the game. "Frank seems almost human when he's away from Tom." she said.

"Yes."

"There's still something faggy though. Have you ever been in that... scene?"

"No." I said. "Sometimes I think I understand it. But I've never been in it."

"I did once," she said. "I'm not sure I knew what I was doing. I suppose I did, though."

"Yes."

"I guess I wanted to know."

"Yes."

"It's funny...."

"Your game." said Frank. He handed me the paddle and sat down. I volleyed with Archy. While we played, Frank and Archy continued a conversation they had been having about angel-fish—which, it seems, have a very delicate and discriminating sex life. Female angel-fish, says Archy, are very cool and will mate only with the male of their choice. Once they have chosen they cannot be mated with any other male. In fact, if the couple is separated after mating there will be no eggs. I expressed interest. For actual mating, I was told, the angel-fish require exactly twenty-four gallons of water and complete isolation. They cannot be watched, and both male and female eat those eggs which appear inferior. I was pretty interested. I do not know if all this is true. But that is what they told me.

Archy and I played a game which I won easily. Ginny had gone back upstairs. We began a second game. I noticed Wilson standing in the doorway, watching us. He did not seem especially wet. He was intent on the game. I nodded to him and began playing hard. My slams had a bite to them. I looked over from time to time to see if Wilson were still there. He watched for a while, then left. Archy was being badly beaten, but he took it with grace. When we finally rested he complimented me and went downstairs to the Men's room.

George came down the stairs and asked to play. He looked tired, but seemed amiable. We volleyed for a long time. I could feel George relaxing as he played. The volleying grew quite professional as we probed and feinted, testing each other's nerves and reflexes. I did not notice at once, but I gradually became aware that Wilson was standing in the doorway again, watching us with great interest. George and I continued volleying. We did not speak, but subtle communication flowed within our form. George had not turned to look, but I knew that he was aware of Wilson.

We continued playing. Several more people entered the room and stopped to watch us play. I was now in excellent form. The paddle had become an extension of my arm. My shots were as easy as pointing a finger. Gradually my consciousness drew inward, more concerned with viscera than with people. I became my own spectator, detached and awe struck, mindless of the people in the room. George, alone, still figured in my thinking, and he was no more than an extension of myself. The rhythm of the ball connected us, drew us close as Gemini, until my viscera encompassed his and we played with one motion.

This is the way the game can be—at its best. I know it, though I have never experienced such a moment since. And then as I turned intuitively to return the ball from where I knew it would be, my eye performed a radial connection with the periphery. The strings connecting us snapped as my consciousness expanded and I hit the ball hard and wrong into the net. What I had seen was Karen, standing where Wilson had stood, her head pivoting with the ball as she looked from George to me to George to me....

"Let's play a game." I said.

George seemed reluctant, "This has been so much fun...." I insisted and we volleyed for serve. As the ball crossed the net for the third time, Benny the art director plucked it out of the air. We looked at him, astonished. He was angry. There was a cut over his left eye.

"No more ping-pong tonight." he said. He looked at George. "Haven't you had enough for one day? You people play your games and see what it leads to? Now go up and get rid of that canvas before somebody else cracks up."

There were at least thirty people watching the game, and they were angry. There were mutterings all around, Benny stood firm.

"That goes for all of you. You've got better things to do." He walked upstairs.

"He means it," George said tiredly. He put down the paddle and went upstairs. The crowd dispersed in knots of two and three. Karen came over to me.

"Well, that's that." I said.

"He's right about one thing." she said. "There's work. God there's work. I've got to go rehearse my quartet now."

"This late?"

"Yes. We're going to Joe Reily's house. You can come...."

"No." I said quickly. "I'm not feeling well. I think maybe I've caught cold. I'll go to bed, I think—try to beat it before it starts."

"Good idea." she said. "Here," she fumbled in her purse, "take these—they're stronger than Bufferin." She handed me two white pills. I thanked her and we separated....

Delirious

I had caught cold—small wonder, considering the physical condition the Army had brought me to. When I woke the next afternoon, I had a high fever and my chest ached. I dressed and went over to the barn where I knew Karen would be practising. Half-way to the barn, I regretted having come. Rain almost hissed when it struck my face. From one of the practice rooms—the one at the end of the ping-pong room opposite the doorway to the exhibition room—I could hear viola music. I knew Karen's sound quite well, and recognized it immediately—warm, delicate, close to the bridge, heavy with vibrato. I thought of opening the door, but then I heard Joe Reily's voice. She was having a lesson and I did not wish to interrupt. From out of one of the practice rooms down the hallway to my left, came Alvin, carrying his violin.

"Good." he said, "I wanted to take a break. How about a game? Of course, maybe you'd rather not...."

"I'm not feeling too good." I said. "Maybe a short volley."

"Oh I didn't really mean a game. More a lesson, I guess. Wait a minute, please." He went back in the practice room and put away his violin. Then he returned and served the ball to me before I had picked up my paddle. "I'm sorry." he said. He said it before he realized that I had actually returned the ball.

We volleyed for a while. He had improved remarkably in three days, and I told him so. It was a mistake. He fluttered and went into a tail-spin. It was several exchanges before he had recovered.

"I've been playing a little with Wilson." he said.

"Is he good?"

Alvin looked as if I had questioned the validity of music. "He's wonderful. Of course...well, he says you can't tell about somebody till you see him playing somebody else who's good. But he's good. He can do anything. He picked up my violin the other night and played a fiddle tune. He could play really well—if he worked at it.... Hey—will you show me how you do your serve? I mean, you don't have to give any secrets, just...."

"Which serve? I have four." It was a bit pretentious, perhaps.

"The backhand one—the one everybody hits off the table."

So I instructed Alvin in the mysteries of the backhand serve—the top-spin serve. We worked on it for half an hour, and he made some progress. Alvin was not, I concluded, totally uncoordinated. He just manifested terrible lapses of attention. His progress now excited him.

"Is that the way real table-tennis players serve?" he said, awe-struck at the thought that he might actually comprehend the mechanics.

"No." I drawled. "Most of em have tricks of their own. One, for instance, might feint like this before serving." (I demonstrated) "Another will keep alternating his serve between top-spin and under-spin." (I served the latter and Alvin flapped it into the net) "You see? I use four serves—two forehand, two backhand. But this one I've shown you is as good as any and better than most. If you vary the speed, you won't ever need another serve."

The door behind me opened and Karen and Joe Reily emerged. Reily saw me first.

"Well," he said, "did you hear? This little girl has an awfully big sound."

He raised his arms to show how big. His left arm whacked into Karen's breast. He laughed, excused himself, and left.

I looked after him. "Time is money." I said.

Alvin thanked me for the instruction and went back to his practice room.

"We'll have to get you on the payroll." said Karen. "There's more teaching out here than in the classrooms. How are you feeling?"

Alvin stuck his head outside the door again. "I haven't forgotten your nickel." he said. "I'll bring it this afternoon."

"Pretty cheap." said Karen. "Is that all you charge?"

"It was for a tip." I said. "I feel pretty bad. How was rehearsal?"

She looked tired. "Ok, I guess." she said.

Automatically, we had begun batting the ball—a reflex. She missed the table and the ball went through the open door into her practice room. I followed after it.

"Come here." I said.

She followed me into the room. I shut the door and flipped the latch-lock. I embraced her and kissed her hard.

"Much better." I said. I kissed her again. "It's been almost a week, Karen...."

It is my opinion that our civilization balances precariously on the edge of darkness. Just as the amoeba surrendered immortality when he decided to specialize and become a paramecium; just as the frog surrendered the pleasures of a lubricant context when he decided to breathe air; just as the little mamma1 traded the victory he had won by eating dinosaur eggs for the cares of a dynastic effort of his own; just as he later stood up and traded balance for a back-ache—so has our civilization surrendered independence for some dubious conveniences.

Now, like a finely tuned violin (so finely tuned, in fact, that the a string requires a special metal tuning-ratchet—two complete turns for one half-tone), our society is more at the mercy of its environment and of its own convolutions than before we began the process.

Someday a fuse is going to blow somewhere within the awesomely complex network of our electrical system. A relay station will overload the interrupted circuit. A surge of power will cascade past startled stagnant switchboxes, blowing more fuses belatedly as it goes. And the entire country will sputter and go out—a massive and perhaps irrevocable breakdown in all communication.

"I know." said Karen. "You must dread going back. But you have another week still...."

I grabbed her roughly and pulled her to the floor. I lay upon her and kissed her passionately.

"I have a rehearsal..." she said.

I kissed her again. She responded with reluctance. I reached beneath her skirt and pulled at her underclothes. Her body began to shudder.

"Here?" she said. "I can't...."

"Here." I almost begged. "Please, Karen...." I did beg.

The environment was not well chosen. The floor of the practice room is covered by one of those damn grass—braided straw—carpets, the texture of which has all the delicacy of burlap. She looked at the dried rug helplessly. She shifted position and touched me roughly with her hands. The wrestling had made me dizzy. My head fell back to the floor, my cheek lacerated by the rug. Karen reclined beside me, perpendicular to me. I could see the caked mud on her tennis shoes. I closed my eyes and began spinning. I breathed rapidly, congested and wheezing. Karen moved on me as a craftsman with a job to get done. My body twitched, then jerked violently. From far inside me vomit came, searing my throat as it passed, exploding finally on the rug.

"I'm sick." I moaned. "Oh God, Karen, I'm sick!"

More vomit—then I lay heaving convulsively till only saliva drooled from my lips. Yet still I heaved for several minutes. Karen, terrified, held my head, murmuring comfort sounds.

"You're burning up." she said. "We've got to get you home. Can you walk?"

I was too miserable to answer. She went to the door, fumbled at the lock, opened it, and called for Alvin. I recollect little of the walk home. I cannot believe that Alvin was of much use. But somehow I did get to bed — and became aware of my environment again only on Sunday morning.

Thus I missed the Friday night concert (which was, by all reports, quite excellent), and the Saturday night party at the White House (during which Julie the cellist told Benny to shove his paint brush up his ass and ride it like a pogo-stick).

Sometime during Saturday a local doctor was called about my condition. I am told that, vaguely responsive to surrounding conversation, I informed the doctor that I had an urgent appointment at the White House. The poor man assumed I was delirious and, as a result, apparently lost some time in his diagnosis. I do not, of course, recall any of this.

He prescribed his special pill remedies for what he called "twenty-four-hour flu", and assured everyone that it was "going round". Pills were stuck into me according to a schedule, vaguely Mayan in its complexity. And they must have had some effect, because — not only was I conscious Sunday morning — but I felt not badly at all. The fever had broken and I was very hungry.

The weather had broken with my fever. Forecasts warned that the break was temporary; nevertheless sun streamed through the colored curtains. I was served a generous breakfast by both George and Karen, who, it seems, had taken turns attending me — a complication of their schedules lovingly endured and executed. The ensuing discussion centered, logically enough, on my health. But the issues, I soon learned, rippled far beyond this center. For Karen and George had a Plan.

The last week of the summer school was now in motion. Starting Monday, the school would ratchet into over-drive until Friday. Although certain formalities would occupy the following week through Wednesday, the practical facts were these: if everybody could survive the tests, rehearsals, paint shortages, and bad tempers until Friday — the summer school would end on a note of triumph rather than disaster. The anxieties of the past week had convinced George and Karen of the need for some wholesome recreation. Although an extra day of work was badly needed, they had determined to sacrifice Sunday. The teeth of the gears were badly worn but perhaps the heavy lubricant of pleasure might keep the wheels from the slipping that would tear.

They had decided then, tentatively — according to the weather and my health — on an expedition to Bashbish Falls, some fifty miles away in the National Forest at the corner of Connecticut, Massachusetts and New York. There would be a barbeque, swimming, perhaps, community wine-drinking, and all attendant festive sports. The question was: could I manage—swathed in blankets, of course, and under loving supervision?

While they talked I began a furtive inventory, of my resources. I tested each muscle of my body. The results were ambiguous. My stomach was now balanced again and my head was cool and clear. But such accessories as sinews and tendons evidenced weakness. As I hesitated, they decided not to go. The others would leave as planned, but they would remain to care for me. Or, one would remain—for I did not require both. Inevitably they began debate on who would stay.

"I feel fine," I said. "Let's go. It sounds like fun."

There was more debate. Did I really mean it? Of course, Bashbish was really beautiful, but it was probably foolish for me to go. One could go again sometime, after all....

"Really," I said, "I want to go."

And the interrupted machinery of preparation began to whirr again.

It was a good idea and they had prepared carefully. The money had been collected; the food was ready—and the wine, and the vehicles. It was a good idea—as well organized as a trip to Pamplona, and nearly as disastrous. Neither weather nor personality can be organized; the failure of the Bashbish Expedition was not the fault of George and Karen.

The sky was cold and clear as we departed. There were seven cars, altogether, packed with merry-makers who were our friends. Seven cars returned that night, carrying the same number of people.

Bashbish Falls, despite its name, is pretty. The National Forest is pretty, too. Broad rock ledges surround the falls and a natural rock-sided pool which is perhaps twenty-five yards in diameter, deep enough for swimming. In two places you can swim directly under the falls—Esther Williams style. The water is always glacier-cold. So too, by the time we arrived, was the air.

I have not the excuse of illness for my reluctance to tell of that trip. I am only reluctant. The trouble may have begun when Ken pretended to throw Alicia into the pool, and accidentally succeeded. Alicia was not amused, and her mood may have worked upon us all. Perhaps the growing tension between Ginny and Ross was what tightened us; or—the rain, a cold intermittent drizzle from noon into the evening.

The incidents of the day were dramatic, and I am not sure why I refuse to re-order them. Bob called Ginny a cock-teaser, for one thing, and Ross hit him. For another, Joe Reily dropped a wine bottle into the pool; and it broke, staining the water. George went in to fish out the pieces of glass, and cut his left arm, which colored the water even more.

I think, perhaps, my interest is naturally disposed toward what does not happen. Then again, I am weary of this story, tired of sorting the thousand things I still do not understand. To give the largest, most reflective judgment on the causes of the Bashbish fiasco—I think an evil spell was put upon our party. By the end of the day Karen, George, and I were still speaking to one another. In this we were unique.

The charcoal hamburgers were good, and so was the corn—not quite done enough for my taste, but hot, anyway. At the end of the barbeque Bob threw the half-empty can of charcoal lighter on the fire and yelled, "Run!" Everyone scattered but George, who grabbed up a blanket and, holding it before him like an asbestos shield, calmly advanced upon the fire. With his foot he kicked away the can before it could explode. I mention this because it was the only thing anybody did with grace that day.

One car ran out of gas on the way back, and another had a flat tire. Two miles outside of Norfolk I began shaking again, and spent the next four days in bed.

The relapse—if it was that, and not simply a new disease—was a peculiar cycle of fever-chill delirium and periods of weak lucidity. Each day I seemed to get better, and each night I was worse again. The pace of the school continued and I was left to myself much of the time, during the day and early evening when I was usually all right. I slept a lot, and read, and wrote occasionally. Karen and George stopped in to talk when they could. Ginny visited me several times.

I say I was lucid, and that is my recollection; yet, to judge from my writing, it was a peculiar lucidity. My discussions with Ginny very much involved my writing, so I suspect that she tolerated a good deal of incoherence. Possibly—a heady flower in a sick room—she caused it.

The rain continued as well as the interpersonal gloom. Ginny and Ross had irrevocably parted. Karen's tan was fading, and she looked terrible. George alone seemed unaffected by the weather. Yet he, too, had his mark—the bandage on his left arm.

But for me it was a pleasant interlude. Ginny and I talked a lot about John Webster. She read the Duchess and went on to The White Devil, and we discussed the plays at length. She was a good listener, and bright enough to stop me when I was foolish. Once she delighted me by saying: "I think you are your own chronicle too much, and grossly flatter yourself."

I agree; I am.

Discussion also verged (inevitably) on Shane, as I explained to her the theological problems of the story. They go something like this:

Shane's divine intervention is initially passive—the assertion of moral force. But moral force, like a gun-fighter, invites challenge. Shane's presence tips the balance so much that the evil angel, Wilson, must be summoned to restore it. And once Wilson arrives, the struggle changes and intensifies. The killing of pigs, the cutting of fences, the trampling of gardens—these give way to murder. If you raise the level from man to angel, you raise the stakes. The divine intervention, then, causes death. And—to complicate the issue further—Shane is an angel out of the Proserpine myth or a Tolstoi parable, who is weary of his role and longs for a human life. He would avoid the guns which are his function. Yet he is a hero; he cannot be less and still retain the place he wishes in the community. Heroes must act. A man conditioned to action cannot avoid a fight. Yet fist-fighting, necessary both for the human respect he needs and for the moral advantage he has brought, sets in motion those causes which force Shane to assume the function he would abandon. Eventually, the result of his human longings and of the inevitabilities of his divine function, Shane must put on his gun again and become the impersonal and perfect machine. It is a fascinating trap.

This much sense I have distilled from my writings of the time. I have condensed considerably and deleted some rather elegant hyperbole. But this is the sense of my lectures as I remember them.

George was with us for one such talk. He was, as I recall it, quite interested in the issues of Shane's problem of participation in human affairs. My theory of the attendant consequences intrigued him, and he seemed most curious about the actual form of these consequences. He posed an interesting question: why, then, must Shane kill humans as well as Wilson? Why, further, if he is perfect, does Shane get wounded? My written reply is as follows:

...so the conflict must move from fists to guns, from the human to the machine, from the New Dispensation to the Old. And vain now appears the dialogue with Marian Starret, who had protested the instruction in gun-use that Shane had given Joey. "A gun is a tool, Marian," Shane had said, "no better, no worse than the man who uses it." "I wish there weren't a gun in the whole valley," she had replied, "including yours, Shane." And thus the positions had locked, each reasonably balancing the other, each true to the spirit and function of its speaker.

But now, in the deadly seriousness of the final show-down, how these lines squirm—like undigested rodents in the belly of a snake. For a gun is a tool, as good as Shane, as evil as Wilson. But for these two who use guns, that moral value is predetermined by the supernatural function of each. Shane becomes his gun, as Wilson becomes his. Each man becomes an extension of the emblem of his function; each man becomes his function.

Were there no other guns in the valley, Shane would not have to recover his carefully wrapped up holster from beneath the blanket roll in the barn. But then, were it not for Shane's code—the divine super-rationality that can believe that a gun is only a tool, were it not for this inhuman simplicity—the crisis could have never been provoked. Wilson's gun could never have appeared.

So Shane straps on his gun, and leaves what he most desires, to confront Wilson and kill him. The concentration he brings to this task makes of him the machine he had not been before. It is also nearly his undoing. For the destruction of Wilson is easy enough. But the consequences of the struggle have reached man, as well.

On earth Evil cannot challenge Good within an entirely neutral arena.

Grafton's saloon is as neutral a place as can be found in the Wyoming Territory, for Grafton is a decent man, and the "rules" have always been to "make things look right to Grafton". Even so, the town has been the setting for conflict, for violence—and violence corrupts. The town is tainted; it is a place of men. And if the balance didn't naturally lean slightly toward Evil, there would have been no need for Shane in the first place.

Preoccupied by his supernatural adversary, Shane, having disposed of Wilson, seems a trifle slower in dispatching Riker (the man who has sold his soul). And it is only Joey's human warning that saves Shane from the hidden third man—the least tainted of the assassins.

And so Shane pays the cost of the angel tempted by earth, and he leaves the carnage with a physical wound of his own—the slight wound of the nearly-perfect Gawain.

And thusly marked, fixed once again in his terrible function, he rides out of the valley to the unfixed, unformed societies of men that lie further west....

I do not recall whether I gave George an answer at the time. That much and more I wrote, but my memory is a little confused and, for all I know, I may have quoted some irrelevancy from the Duchess.

These four days occur to me now only as a calm interlude, a series of relaxed talking that changes order each time I think of it. It was a confused time, but one of warmth. I was cared for well and my condition improved. By Thursday evening I had completely shaken the illness, and felt only weak.

I'll Kill Him

It was the evening before the performance of Karen's quartet. It was also—though no one at Norfolk could see it—the evening of the full moon. This is more fact than justification.

The tensions of her work and her concern for me had allowed Karen little sleep for several nights. I was out of bed and dressed when she came in. She looked very tired.

"I'm cured," I announced.

"Good." she said. "I'm glad someone is."

"Just one more day—" I said, "you can take it. JD always said you were the toughest chick in town."

She muttered something.

"What?"

She sat on the bed and removed her shoes, "I said, 'Good old JD.'" she said.

"Is there something I can do to help you?"

She muttered something.

"What?"

"I said, 'Now!' All week I'm out of my mind with work and nursemaiding you, and now you want to help me!"

"I didn't mean to get sick."

She smiled. "I know. I'm sorry. I'm just awfully tired and I'm not playing well. It's going to be awful—I know it."

"Oh, come on—" I said, "as Joe Reily would say, 'every cloud has a silver....'"

"Just cut it out about Joe! Ok? He's a great teacher. Ok?"

"Ok."

I sat down in the chair and spilled the ashtray, "Do you have to keep messing up the room?" she said. "I've got enough to do without cleaning up all the time."

"I'm sorry." I said.

She began picking up the cigarette butts. I reached down to help her. I touched her shoulder. "Karen...."

She shook off my hand and continued cleaning up the ashes. Her hair was wet; strands were pasted against her neck.

"Is it still raining hard?" I said.

"No. It stopped about supper-time."

"The reason I asked..." I paused. "The reason I asked was I saw your hair was wet, and I just wondered if it was still raining."

She turned her head. "I was swimming."

"Yes—well, you see, that didn't occur to me because you didn't bring in your suit—in fact it's still over there by the duffel bag; so naturally...."

She stood up and replaced the filled ashtray on the bedside table by the chair. "None of us had suits. We needed a break, so we went swimming. It was dark...."

"At Reily's?"

"Yes—look, if you're going to start on him again...." She began to undress. "I'm not in the mood. I'm just not in the mood for that."

I sat back in the chair. "Don't tell me he's never tried." I said.

She laughed and mumbled something under her jersey.

"What? What's funny?"

She emerged smiling. It was the fixed smile of her least attractive role. "I'm laughing because you said, 'don't tell me he's never tried.' So I won't."

I stood up quickly and accidentally knocked over the ashtray again. Her eyes flashed. "I thought I told you...."

"And I told you!" I yelled. "He's old enough...." I stopped and began pacing.

"Stop pacing," she said. "Calm down. You said, 'don't tell me he's never tried', so...."

"I know what I told you. I distinctly remember it. It is etched indelibly in my memory. Has the sonofabitch ever tried to make you?"

She did not answer. She sat on the bed and began un-zipping her skirt.

"Answer me. Has the sonofabitch.... Answer me. Goddamn it".

"Of course." she said placidly. "Everybody does. That's the whole game, isn't it?"

"Have you ever been unfaithful to me, Karen?"

"I don't think I'll answer that." she said. She removed her skirt. "I don't like the word—for one thing. For two weeks you've been playing with that whore...and I don't think I'll answer you. Oh that scored, I see."

"She's not a whore." I said.

"Oh—yes? Well, Joe's a sweet, warm guy and he's terribly lonely. I don't think it's so bad if he wants me. I kind of like the idea."

"Don't defend him." I said. My voice was soft.

"Look—" she said, "all men try. Nobody minds...."

"I don't." I said. "I don't try. My friends...."

She laughed harshly. "Your friends!" She turned her body and started to lie down. Her shoulders twisted mid-way, and off-balance, awkward, in a wild reverse hay-maker her voice slammed at me across her shoulder: "JD was all over me every time he saw me—and you think Joe Reily's evil or something."

"No." I said. "I don't believe it."

She lay still and covered her eyes with her hand. "My eyes hurt." she said. "Can't you turn off the overhead light?"

"I don't believe it." I said, I was still standing in the center of the room.

"The light..." she said, "please...."

I switched off the overhead light.

"Look—" she said, "we went swimming a few times. I like to swim. It's no crime."

I crossed to the bed and sat beside her, intervening between the bed-lamp and her face. She turned away from me, lying on her side in the shadow.

I touched her shoulder gently. "But he's my friend...." I said, "he introduced us. He said...."

"He'd made me, baby—he could afford to."

"No." I said. "No. The grass...by the Sacred Path...after the movie...."

"It wasn't the first." Her voice was muffled in her arm, remote and strange. "Didn't you think it was a little easy?"

"No." I said. "No."

She sat up violently and stared straight ahead at the blank white wall. "You're such a Romantic... that's what attracted me.... You sentimentalize everything. You think that was so sweet and loving and wonderful— try being on the bottom sometime! See how nice it is getting layed in the grass! It was wet and itchy."

"You said you liked it."

"You—I liked you...God knows why, after that performance in the Ledge."

I began almost to cry—no sobbing, no heaving, no sound, not even moisture—just a tight rhythmic constriction. I lay back beside her. She turned her body to me and threw her arms around me, sobbing: "Oh God! Oh I'm sorry! I didn't mean that...I didn't mean any of it."

I couldn't speak. I tried, but my throat was tight.

"I never went with him again...honest. It was just once. It was before you...what difference does it make...?"

I tried to explain. "It's just the grass...." I said. "You're right...I senti-mentalize...it meant a lot to me.... It's silly, though. You're right. I don't care about JD. He knows what he lost. I'm glad—I guess."

I sat up and lit a cigarette, Karen's face was in the pillow.

"How many people have you slept with?"

She moved her face clear of the pillow. "You mean all together...all at the same time...?" She made a small giggle.

"Seriously, Karen...."

"Oh—about eighty-four...counting the women, too...if you add the an-imals...."

"How many?"

There was a long silence. Her body was a rigid line, straight as a table edge. Something broke and her form grew soft. There was a long silence during which I drew heavily on the cigarette.

"All right...three." she said.

I reached down and righted the ashtray on the floor. I stubbed out the cigarette. "JD," I said, "and I, and...." I swung my legs on to the floor and walked to the duffel bag in the corner of the room. I began pawing through the duffel bag.

"What are you doing?"

I pulled out my sheathed hunting knife and stuck it in my back pocket. I picked up my army fatigue jacket and put it on.

"Where are you going?"

"To see Joe Reily."

She left the bed and came toward me. She was wearing only a bra and a half-slip. "Why?" she said.

"I'm going to kill him." (Do you hear me, Reily, Joe Reily, Joe? Read me very carefully, for I strike through my mask: This much passion remains to me—if I ever see you again, you Dirty Stinking Old Man, I will kill you.)

Karen stood still. "You're crazy."

"Yes."

"You can't kill him. He's a great teacher...and he's nice.... You can't kill people."

She put her hand to her face. Her eyes were brown and they looked straight at you. "You're crazy. You're going to do it. I should have known... at that movie. You're insane."

"I hit that guy because he insulted you."

"Because he insulted Marian, you mean...a character in a stupid movie...you're sick—you don't know what's real...and now.... It must be that whore...Ginny...that's why. Not me. Never me...."

Half way through her speech my arm began drifting toward her. At the end of my arm a fist appeared. I watched it curiously. It had formed out of four fingers and a thumb, acting in concert. And now the knuckles which had not been there a moment before made shadows on my wrist, I studied the smooth motion of my arm, and comprehended its purpose. I signaled a retraction of orders, but was able only to alter the direction of the motion. The punch caught her on the shoulder and knocked her down. She fell back slowly, her slip fluttering like a flag of truce. Her elbow struck the radiator cap and knocked it loose. Like the fine spray of a French fountain, steam began cascading upwards, filling the air, hanging in the air, buoyant—molecules in random collision. The radiator was filled with snakes. The noise shook me.

I leaped to her. She cowered, threw up her hand protectively, "Don't hit me."

"No...oh God, no....Oh I'm sorry...oh...please, God...are you hurt?"

She held up her left arm. The steam had seared a line across her wrist.

"You hurt me." she said, "You burned me."

I kissed her face and hair. "I'm sorry...oh forgive me...I'm sorry."

The hissing roused me again. I grabbed the cap and jammed it back on, intentionally blistering my fingers. I turned back to her.

"You had to hurt." she said. Her voice was like a child's. "You're violent.... You hurt me."

"I know.... I know...please forgive me."

"And you were going to kill...." She held up her hands. They were sooty from the ashes on the floor. A shred of tobacco clung to her palm. She stared at it, then at me. She rubbed her face, streaking it. "Don't hurt me...please...don't kill me...."

Every so many million years the earth's polarity reverses. They have found evidence for this in the ocean beds.

Her voice dropped several levels. "You fool!" she snarled. "It wasn't Joe Reily—you fool! It was George! That's right, baby, go kill George!"

So you see. Gentle Reader, what is obvious may also be true.

Picture now an early morning mist hanging low over the ruins of an ancient abbey. A woman kneels upon the ground, her white gown spreading out before her—a gauzed and tangible extension of the mist. The man looks down upon her, smiling. The first gold of the morn has settled upon his hair. He speaks:

"Let us make noble use of this great ruin. These wretched eminent things leave no more fame behind them than should one fall in a frost and leave his print in snow. As soon as the sun shines it ever melts both form and matter. Come—I forgive you."

"Thank you." she cries. "Oh thank you."

Uh uh.

She had risen to her feet. Her sooty face was a stranger's. "Why not?" She hissed. "Why not? What the hell have you been doing with Ginny?"

I was frozen somewhere near the center of the room. "But I didn't." I said. "It's not fair. I could have—but I didn't. It's just not fair."

I shook my head slowly, staring at the floor, tracking an unfamiliar motion. "Did you make love often?" I said.

"Lots—all the time."

"Was it good? Did you enjoy it?"

"Yes. I liked it a lot—very much."

I fell across the bed and began screaming—nerve slicing, soundless.

Karen sat on the bed beside me. "I'm sorry about Ginny...I thought...."

I shook my head. My fist was jammed in my mouth, my tongue licking at the blisters. "Karen...." I tried to speak.

"No." she said. She was very tired. "No. It was nice, and you'll try to make it dirty. I'm sorry now—but it was nice."

I took my hand from my mouth. "I want to understand." I said. "Please help me understand."

"It's late." She said. She lay beside me. "I'm tired and so sorry...." She switched off the bed-lamp.

"Since I came...?" I said.

"Oh, no...before.... What's the point? Let's just...." Her voice fell soft and insubstantial. Then, "I was so worried. I wasn't making it. And you didn't care. All you could talk about was your trouble with the Army. But he understood. I didn't know at first. It was a sexual thing, but I didn't think about it. He was a good friend. I was a little confused. He's so much like you. Half the time I thought he was you. But I did it all. He never asked me, I just kind of wandered around in a daze—not knowing where I was half the time...who I was, I mean. And he's like you, only not so violent. So all at once I was with him in his bed and it was nice. I was cracking up. It helped me. And then you came and I got scared. I knew you wouldn't understand...." And she began crying softly—poison flowed from her, healing and silent.

I put my arms around her. "I do understand." I said. "It's all right. Nothing's changed. It's all right...." And I repeated these words like an incantation till we were both asleep.

This I did, or should have done, or both....

I woke late, exhausted and aching. Karen was lying beside me, her eyes open, watching my face.

"Hi." I said. "Good morning."

"Hi," she said. Her face was puffed and creased by the pillow. "Do you hate me?" she said.

"Gee—I don't think so. Let me see...I think, maybe, I love you. By the way—tell me who you love."

She shook her head. "I don't know." she said miserably. "I'll go make coffee."

"Yes." I said. "Why don't you do that."

She dressed and crossed the room.

"By the way...."

She turned at the door.

"By the way," I drawled, "Ah'm kind a slow, but ah see things sometimes. And ah know if anything happened to me that you'd be took care of better than ah could do it. Ah never thought ah'd hear myself sayin' a thing like that, but ah reckon this is a good time to lay things bare."

She did not answer.

I was still clothed from the night before. I inverted procedure and took off my fatigue jacket. I went downstairs to the kitchen. Wind was howling like a wolf not far off, thence at the door, and rain beat hard against the window. She served the coffee. "I've got a rehearsal." she said. "It's the last one." She looked at her hand. The red mark across her wrist had turned white.

"How is it?" I said, "I'm awfully sorry."

"I know. It's not too good. It hurts. Oh well, I was going to play bad anyway. It's an excuse now. What are you going to do?"

"I think I'll just brood around the house. No point in risking my precious health out there. I think I'll just brood around."

She put on her coat, "Everything's forgivable, Dick, in my book, anyway."

"Ah, yes," I said, "but your's is a loose-leaf book."

She laughed. "That's good." she said. "You'd better write it down." She put her hand on the door knob.

"Karen, I had a dream. We were in George's car up at the top of the driveway. You were driving. I warned you the brakes were bad, but you kept driving too fast—down the hill toward the house. I started yelling, 'put on the hand-brake!' I yelled it several times. You didn't do anything. Finally I reached over you and pulled it myself. The car finally stopped just before the house. We broke down a fence—that isn't there—but that's all the damage. I screamed at you: 'why didn't you put on the emergency brake?' You said, 'You kept calling it the "hand-brake". I didn't know what you meant.'"

Karen opened the door. It was very cold outside. "I guess that shows we're not communicating too well." She said.

"I guess so." I said. "It was really vivid."

"I'll think about it." She said.

"Yes, so will I."

She left and closed the door behind her.

"Inevitability" is a word I do not much like, though I use it now and then. Like "potential", it is a word one is simply stuck with—meaningless, but expressive. I went into the living room and sat on the couch. Here I began for the first time what has since become a life's project. It was not very well organized—that thinking—but I do not have to tell you that it was thorough. And the word "inevitability", or one of its grammatical variants, kept coming to my mind. I was relaxed, I think. There is comfort in inevitability—so long as you can believe it.

I thought for a long time. Then I picked up George's guitar and played it for a while. Then I put it back and thought again. I went upstairs to retrieve my notebook, I brought it to the living room and wrote down the "loose-leaf book" line, as Karen had suggested. I skimmed the pages I had already written, and re-read the dialogue of our first date, I jotted in a note: "work in line from Shane after fight—K tells both JD and me, 'it was brutal and ugly, and you were both magnificent.'"

I re-read the lines about responsibility. I inserted another note: "recall Ferdinand's death-line—as Prince Ferdinand dies, he says with the illumination of sanity which death has brought him, 'Whether we fall by ambition, blood, or lust—/ Like diamonds we are cut with our own dust.'" It is my favorite line from my favorite play.

> Then I stood tall and terrible as a Prince, and ranted to the walls:
>
> That I might toss her palace 'bout her ears,
>
> Root up her goodly forests, blast her meads.
>
> And lay her general territory as waste
>
> As she hath done her honors.

My voice rumbled through the empty house; from living room to dining room to kitchen the timbre rolled, dying finally somewhere, probably, in the bath room. Alone as I was, it seemed a trifle inappropriate. And I subsided laughing. All this required hours.

Late in the afternoon I took the sheathed hunting knife from my hip pocket. I removed the sheath and examined the blade. What, after all, was one to do? The grace of the blade's curve was comforting. I examined it carefully.

I heard the kitchen door opening and Karen calling my name.

"In here." I called.

She came into the living room. She stopped and stared. "What's the knife out for?"

"Nothing melodramatic—I was writing a poem, that's all."

"But why the knife?"

"The poem's about the knife. I'll tell it. Ok?"

"Yes."

"My Dad gave me this knife when I first went to Scout camp. Do you remember how Prince Ferdinand says, 'this was my father's poniard; I'd be loath to see it look rusty....'?"

She nodded.

"You see how neatly it a11 fits...with the sex, too?"

She nodded.

"Well—that's not all the poem, though. When he gave me the knife, he also took me aside and had a little talk with me. He said that since I was going off to camp, I ought to be prepared for something. That I knew about sex and had been told everything, and that it was normal etc., and nothing to worry about—but at camp I'd run into guys who would get a little nasty about sex, because everybody didn't know that it was beautiful and normal, and I shouldn't get upset about it if some of them were that way, but I should pity them and forget about it. And the first day I was there, I went fishing. And I cut my hook out of a fish I had caught. And I got fish blood all over the blade. And I scrubbed and scoured and honed all summer and I couldn't get the stain out and I never could and here— you can still see it. And that's the poem."

"I think it has possibilities."

"No. That's it. What I said—that's the poem."

"Oh, that's it?"

"Yes."

"You don't usually leave them so loose."

"The first night I met you I was writing a poem. And I thought it was somehow fitting...."

"The last night, you mean?"

"Yes. But that's the best I could do under the circumstances, I'm sorry."

She nodded. She had not taken off her coat. "I came to tell you I was going to supper. The concert's at 8:00. We go on first. Are you going to come?"

"I don't know yet."

"I see. There's a party afterwards in the barn. They've been decorating all day. It's pretty. It might be fun."

"Oh, good idea." I said. "By the way, where have you been sleeping since I've been sick? On the couch?"

"No. Look—I told you. Since you've been here, it's stopped. I mean, we just slept."

"Yes—well, I think that does it. You see, I'm just not very... sophisticated."

Karen sat down opposite me, beside the bookcase. She leaned forward, putting her hands on her knees. "It happens." she said. "It happens to everybody. We just have to realize that, and go on as if it hadn't. I've been thinking about it. We're not special. It's...too bad. But it happens to everybody."

It was her finest hour. And this was my civilized response:

"Yes, I always accepted that possibility, but I just never thought you'd do anything irrevocable. I mean, Jesus! How much trouble is it to keep your pants on? I'd have thought it was less trouble than taking them off."

She ignored the latter sentiment and made one more try: "Nothing's irrevocable...."

I made no answer.

"...unless you think so." she added. "I guess you do."

She got up and went to the kitchen. I heard the door open, and my better sense mobilized me. I ran to the door and called after her: "This is a hell of a way to end things!"

She turned. "Go and write a better one." she said, and ran up the path.

I raced into the living room. I seized the knife and flung it to the floor. I fell upon the couch, screaming and shaking. My tear-less passion finally exhausted me and I slept for several hours.

Zenobia

It was after 8:00 when I awoke. I had missed her concert. The living room was dark. I stared out the window for a while, watching the rain fall past the street lights.

What is expected is no more bearable because it is expected. Have you seen pictures of Don Larsen's Perfect game? The expression of rage on Dale Mitchell's face? Mitchell was the final out. As the third strike passed him, he screamed.

My rage was now rested and logical. I thought of my dealings with Ginny, and I cross-examined myself. One must, after all, be fair.

Many pages ago I said that I could dazzle the reader if he let me. I chuckled and went on, leaving the joke unexplained. It is a rather pedantic joke. Perhaps I was wise to let it rest. But, well—in Elizabethan vocabulary "let" means "hinder". The semantic motion from hinder to allow may be the motion of morality. At any rate, troubled by a problem of the heart, I now began to put my brain in order. I turned on a light and wrote the following in my notebook:

> The similarity between Christ's admonition "let
> him who is without sin cast the first stone" and
> the "facts" of psychology might be represented
> as the moral issue of our age. It can be physio-
> logically demonstrated and measured that the
> thought of action produces minute muscle responses
> corresponding to that action. To think, then, is
> to some degree to act. The issues of responsibility
> are grave.

Yet Christ's teaching that thought of adultery

is adultery, was no more than the same plea for

mercy that he made at the stoning. It is unlikely

that he would have insisted upon exact correspondence.

There is a tenuous, but significant difference

between lusting and committing adultery:

1. lust

2. voluntary lust (refusal to block thinking)

3. voluntary and prolonged consideration of action

4. numerous stages and degrees of mixed passive and active steps toward the action.

5. preliminary love-making — decision still not irrevocable

6. love-making

7. repetition....

The pen shook from my hand. I was in their house—the house of their...repetitions. The walls and floors, chairs, couches, beds oozed the fragrance of my betrayal. I ran from room to room, downstairs, upstairs, shrieking: Go to. Mistress, Tis not your whore's milk shall quench my wild fire, but your whore's blood! I yelled it several times. Then I stood before his bedroom door, breathing hard. His door had not been opened by my shouting; nor would I enter it. I spoke to the door and my speech was calm: "No." I said. "It is you." I walked downstairs. I picked the knife up from the floor, sheathed it, and returned it to my hip pocket. There is no telling how the earth's averages were affected, but polarity had reversed again—twice within twenty-four hours. I had decided to kill George.

I rushed out the back-door and staggered under the impact of wind and rain. I stood uncertain. To return to the house was to risk madness, I thought. There was George's car in the driveway. Singularly appropriate. I opened the car door. The keys were on the floor near the seat. Not even Raskolnikov had been better provided. I started the car, and drove the long way round, up the dirt road which curved its winding way to the back of the barn. I drove fast; the mud was slippery and I drove without a thought for the fact. My mind was on more practical matters: The soft, sensual sound of ripping canvas, the symbolic execution—rejected. The hard, twisting stab into a muscled back—rejected. The difficulty of frontal assault, weak from illness, against a stronger, larger man—accepted.

A figure loomed in the road ahead. I slammed the brakes, barely missing her. It was Ginny. The scare had made her slip and fall. I opened the door and went to her.

"Are you Ok?"

She nodded. The rain had matted her hair, and her face was dirty where the mud had splashed her. She shivered, drew back and pointed behind me. I turned, Bob was running at me. He had been following her. He had a piece of wire in his hand. His eyes were quite mad.

"I'm going to kill you!" he screamed. "You've had her for the last time."

I put one hand behind me at my back pocket and held the other out before me. "Don't be a fool." I said. "I don't want to fight you."

His momentum had carried him to within a yard of me. He stopped, his heels skidding off-balance in the mud. He fell back on to the road. The fall stunned him. Then it enraged him. He got to his feet, skidded again, staggered and kept upright. The wind was shrieking now—gale volume. His words were torn, washed from his lips as he formed them. It was almost funny. He repeated himself several times, louder, as loudly as he could scream. It was absurdly important for him to have his say.

"Everybody's had that cunt but me! You cock-sucker, I'm going to kill you!"

I stepped back from him. He was the wrong one. I nearly wept. He lunged for me, tearing at my face with his free hand, groping for the hold he could use to bring the wire around. His fingers raked my face. Slippery with rain and blood, I pushed him off with my left arm. I tore the sheathed knife from my pocket with my right hand. He came at me again. I stepped aside, trying to rip off the sheath. But my tennis shoes slipped and I fell heavily back on to the grass and wet pine needles. He was on me before I could move. His hands were above my face. I blinked my eyes clear, twisted suddenly and brought the knife down sharply on the side of his head. He cried out and fell to the side. I raised the knife again and, holding it by the sheathed blade, slugged him again with the handle. He lay still. Blood ran from his hair-line. I lay there breathing hard. Ginny was at my side.

"Is he dead?"

She poked at him. "He's just knocked out. Are you Ok?"

I held up my right hand. The blisters had torn open. My hand poured blood even as the rain washed it. I picked up my knife with my left hand and awkwardly inserted it into my right hip pocket. I stood up.

"Oh! your face!"

"It's all right." I said. "Get in the car."

We both got in the car. I backed the car around into the grassy slope. I jammed the lever into first gear and made the turn, chewing up the turf behind me. I drove fast, retracing my route until the turn-off into town.

"Where are we going?" Ginny asked.

"You knew about George and Karen." I said.

"Yes."

"You never told me."

"I tried to...everyone knew...it was hard back there...I saw them once—
it was hard for me...."

We drove in silence.

"Where are we going?"

"For a swim." I said.

When we came to the chain across the Toby road I speeded the car
and smashed through, losing both headlights. The chain held, but the left
wooden post pulled free, lashing against the side of the car as we passed.
A yard higher, and it would have shattered the windshield, perhaps de-
capitating us. Ginny said nothing. I drove to the edge of the beach.

"Get out." I said.

She left the car. She stood on the beach. I walked toward her slowly.

"Take off your coat." I said.

She took off her coat and handed it to me. I threw it into the car. She
never moved. The sky was entirely black. The lake was roaring. Methodically I began tearing off her clothes. I tore off every shred of wool and
cotton and lace. I grabbed her arm and led her into the water. I pulled her
down into the water and lay upon her. She shivered as the water struck
her, but she did not resist. I could not see her face. I thrust her legs up
high, like a duck on the shallow water. I forced her back against the sand,
and (yes) I fucked her.

When I was finished I helped her up and led her back to the car. She
put on her coat and sat beside me, shivering. I turned the car around and
silently in absolute darkness drove her to her house. I stopped the car,
went around to her side, and opened the door for her. I helped her out.
She was still shivering. I closed the door and returned to my side. I started
the engine. She came around to my side and started to speak.

"Never's a long time." I said and drove away. Alas Zenobia....

Beaten

I chose the winding road again, the soft mud-slick way around up to the barn. I did not drive fast without the headlights. Rather, I sensed the road, enjoyed it as I drove. When I had reached the barn I stopped the car and sat there for a time. My body was shaking badly. I waited for the shaking to subside. I reached automatically for a cigarette. But the pack was a disintegrated mess of fibre and tissue. The knife was still in my pocket, but my right hand could no longer grip. And I was tired—more tired than I had ever been before. Still the shaking, and I felt ebbing from me the last trickle of whatever nerve tonic had taken me this far.

The barn was lighted in every room but the loft. I could hear the music and laughter of partying. My intentions were ambiguous. I wearily walked from the car to the door of the barn. I slipped several times during those ten yards. When I reached the building it took me several minutes to pull open the door. I walked into the Men's room and tried to wash my face. The soap tormented my hand so that I almost fainted. I leaned over the sink and let the water pour over my head till I was conscious again. I opened the window, pushing it with my left hand. The wind worked upon me. It felt cool and pleasant. I looked out at the rain and seemed to see a thing armed with a rake. It was the Gardener, for reasons of his own cabalistically digging in the storm on a Friday night. It was the touch of insanity, but I did not even wonder at it. I closed the window and walked up the stairs. I had considered the problem of my appearance, but I was not noticed. A table-tennis game was in progress and I was another spectator, standing in the stairway.

The party had been going for at least two hours, I later learned. It had spilled into the ping-pong room as couples had entered to rest from the writhing which passed for dance on this the last Friday of Norfolk. There had been some ping-pong playing, sporadic scenes of awkwardness and fun. And these had passed to the greater hilarity of mixed doubles which had dominated the table for the next hour. As the pleasures of the dance further palled, as the quarrels of drink increased, a kind of impromptu tournament had taken shape. The quality of play had improved; the fun of it had diminished to the serious business that sport can be. The doubles teams had grown homogeneous and skillful. Eventually, the form had passed to the implacability and cold precision of single's play. When George and Wilson ultimately faced each other, word spread fast to the adjoining room. By the time I reached the top of the stairway, they had been volleying for ten minutes. There were nearly sixty spectators jammed around the edges of the room.

Here, then, was the game and audience I would have given anything for, the chance which Benny had cheated me of a week ago. And even had the tone of the room permitted a challenge from me, my hand was as crippled as my brain. Wilson, then, was to be my champion, and God alone may know how ludicrous I found this fact.

They played as I have sometimes played, understated in the calm assurance of their mutual worth and respect for that worth. The volleying was pure pleasure for the aficionado. There was nothing fancy, nothing spectacular. What probing went on was of the mind and nerve. Skills were assumed and not seriously tested. Yet even those in the room for whom table-tennis was no more than a recollected release from the nervousness of a long ago high school canteen—even those could sense the professional brilliance of the play they watched. While following the ball, my eyes would sweep the room, occasionally, and I would see on faces I had not much noticed before—stark recognition of a thing superbly done. It was exhibition table-tennis, without glamor, without flamboyance—a calm and elegant ritual of rhythm. Most of the volleys were long. The interruptions were placement perfections or minor fractional misses. At no time did the ball strike the net. And in my fascination I began to forget. My consciousness narrowed to the green-topped arena where two men enjoyed the best that can be enjoyed—a connection of self which cooperates and competes in one simultaneous experience of rhythmed ordered motion. I joined the others in the room and watched. They volleyed, altogether, perhaps half an hour. And no one left the room.

Without comment Wilson began the volley for serve, and took it on a fine placement at the right corner. He smiled as George flipped the ball to him. Wilson examined the ball closely and placed it on the table. He turned and beckoned to Alvin, who, squire-like, produced for him a small canvas sack. Wilson took the sack and handed Alvin the paddle. Wilson opened the sack and drew forth a black foam-paddle, smooth and thin. He tossed the sack to Alvin, then rubbed the ball beneath the new paddle. He fit the paddle to his hand as one might draw on a glove. He glanced behind, checking his space. He stepped back two yards from the table edge and served.

The serve was low and hard, a top-spin serve to the back-hand side.

George retreated before the serve and came up with it, not very strong, but accurate to Wilson's back-hand. Wilson stepped to his fore-hand side and slapped back-handed at the ball, a hard slam that skidded from the table as George scrambled back to position. George returned it, fore-hand, down the side—weak, but, again, tactically superb. Wilson balanced and then struck fore-hand, slapping at the ball—a side-spin slam indulged in only by foam-paddle experts, mercilessly effective. It was hard and it spun off the table as if the table were, itself, foam. George barely touched the slam.

"One-love," said Wilson.

He poised and served again, the same serve to the same place. George was ready and hooked the ball, just missing, 2-0. Wilson served again, top-spin to George's fore-hand, hard, but higher than before. George hooked his return again—a pretty placement just over the net. Wilson swooped in but over-shot. 2-1. The next two serves were repetitions of the last, high and hard to George's fore-hand. On the first, George chopped down hard, spinning the ball wildly backward as it struck. Wilson adjusted and placed his return. George chopped again and Wilson compensated—another neat placement. George's return was slightly high and hung briefly before Wilson slap-slammed it out of sight. Wilson's last serve was the highest of the series. George seemed to hesitate and finally hooked it into the net. 4-l, Wilson.

George was the favorite, of course. Yet the performance thus far seemed to have awed the audience. There had been the usual sounds of breath, but no cheers, few murmurs even. As George prepared to serve someone said, "Go get him, George". But it was a breach of taste and even the speaker seemed to realize the fact.

My own absorption was very nearly complete. I had not been watching personalities for five serves. I had been examining tactics. Wilson's serve was good, but not excellent. He had won four points from George's only weakness—failure to slam. Wilson's slam was marvelous; even against a fast-reflex scrambler like George, Wilson could score on his second or third slam. So long as Wilson could keep the ball high with impunity, George's best returns would lack sufficient spin to prevent Wilson from slamming. George's hesitation on the last serve had evidenced a similar reasoning, I felt. George had considered a slam of his own, but had rejected the idea. To stay even, George—lacking a slam—would have to dominate the table by playing in close with short, high-spin placements near the net and sides. Against a strong player like Wilson, it would be difficult to take the table. The power of Wilson's drives would have to be received in close, perhaps over the table. Yet it seemed the only way, and might, I thought, frustrate Wilson to advantage.

George followed the script with care. His first serve was a beauty, curling over the net in close and off the table. Wilson reached the ball but hit the net. The next serve came irritatingly short to the other side and Wilson again missed. 4-3. George now played a psychological trump. He drove his serve hard and fast to the far edge of the table. Wilson had moved in slightly and was caught. His return floated high across the net. George hooked it. Wilson slammed. And George had lost a point he should have had—again, the weakness of his offense. George returned to the safe, cute serve. Wilson was ready and caught it well. But George's return was again in tight. Wilson ticked the net and the ball dropped back to his side.

Wilson pounced on the next serve, leaning far over to slap it hard. George's thighs were pressed tight against the table; his paddle did not even move as it scooped the ball, almost at the bounce, and returned it with the force of Wilson's own slam. It was a reflex shot and it put Wilson on defense for the first time. He had to scramble back to return what was as good as a slam. George held the table and kept placing his shots. It was a magnificent volley. Wilson scrambled for some seven returns, but George finally put away the point. Applause spontaneously burst from every corner of the room.

Wilson's next series of serves was like his first—higher and higher, a challenge to a non-existent slam. The exchanges were crisp, but George was over-manned. Of the two points he scored, one was an over-shot slam that Wilson should have made with ease. At the service exchange the score was 8-7, Wilson.

Now George stepped back from the table and crouched low as he served, moving rapidly to the table as soon as he had released the ball. His serve spins were virtuoso pieces. But Wilson handled them. The volleys were long and the drama high—both men tight near the table, struggling for balanced possession of the field. Wilson took the series and prepared to serve, leading 11-9.

George's white shirt was now stained under his arms. It was hard work. I wondered if this long-volley play he excelled in were not costing him energy. It had occurred to me during the last series that Wilson's foam-paddle might be unsettling George—from lack of sound more than from speed or spin. George had undoubtedly played against foam before, but the silence of the foam-paddle can disturb rhythm. George's splendid reflexes had seemed, not so much slower in the last exchanges as, perhaps, vague. This was hyper-criticism, of course; most of the placements had been perfect.

George now balanced himself, set to receive. His eyes were eager and there was no sweat on his face. He held his hands close together and I became aware of the bandage on his left arm. As Wilson served, I saw George's hands—artist's hands...his hands. I dredged up some emotion.

This serve was very high. George hesitated briefly, and then slammed it hard, fore-hand. Breath hissed around me. Wilson returned the slam weakly to George's back-hand. George stiffened and blasted the ball, back-hand, as hard a slam as I had seen.

I have joined debate from time to time on the respective merits of offense and defense as total styles of play. My opinion has usually been that no one can adequately defend against a perfect offense. The point is moot; but here, suddenly, the issue had vanished. This was not to be, after all, the classic problem put to test. For George could slam, and his slam was excellent. Shock rolled round the room like the echo of thunder. And in the ensuing confusion of murmur and rustle all eyes turned to George. All but mine.

For then I saw it. It was mine alone. The others were turning.... My eyes were fixed on Wilson and I saw it. I saw the whole man move, all of him, in a single flashing instant. I saw the head lead and the body swing as he scooped up the ball. I saw the smile split his face like lightening, and the eyes blaze with its reflection. I saw his fingers hook like predatory claws about his weapon as he prepared for battle—a grim and only barely sig-naled indication of the stakes. And George, I am persuaded, saw it, too. For I wrenched my eyes from Wilson to follow his serve and saw George's defiant figure. He lashed at the ball savagely and drilled it to Wilson's back-hand. And Wilson did not retreat, but smote it harder yet. The ball was a blur, but George could see it. He shifted his feet and leaned into his slam, throwing his whole magnificently muscled weight upon the ball. Wilson stepped to the side and slapped at an object I could not see, and put away the shot before George's body had completed its graceful thrust.

There was no applause; the violence of the exchange had shocked. The muscles of my throat tightened and choked me. I felt the humiliation of an amateur confronted with skill beyond his imagination, let alone his reflexes. I could not even bear the shield for these giants. My arrogance! In the emotion of the moment, I felt guilty for ever having played in the same room. I raised my eyes and saw Karen across the room. She, too, was shaken. I worked my throat and chewed and spat down my bitterness. "Get him, Wilson" I urged silently, "he's your's now. Get him."

Wilson served. The serve was low and vicious. George played it as if the ball had been floating high—leaped on it and crushed it back. Wilson stood his ground. They hammered mightily, George drove hard, a perfect slam, splitting off the corner, crazy and venomous. Wilson's body coiled and sprung. His arm swept out before him as he dived to the side, flicking at the ball he should not even have touched. His momentum carried him into the crowd which shrank from him. He pushed himself off the wall and was back again, balanced and ready. But there was no need. His slam had crossed the table, glancing for the point George could not prevent.

Three more times Wilson served. Three more times with feudal violence the ball was blasted between them. Three times more Wilson drove home the point. The score was 15-10 George's serve. And my revenge was near.

George took the ball and examined it. His face was pale and the mus-cles of his mouth were tight. He served cunningly, a heavy ball that wob-bled near the net. Wilson's eyes glittered. He coiled his paddle around the ball and slammed for the score past George's hands. George retrieved the ball, served again—an even tighter, better serve; and Wilson exorcised it. 17-10.

George's shoulders sagged as he picked up the ball. He was tired. He stood holding the ball, breathing hard. And then Wilson held up his hand for time, put down his paddle, and reached into his jacket pocket for a cigarette. He lit it slowly with insolently deliberate grace. The battle was over; the butchery was now to come. I looked at George. He had been out-classed from the beginning, as mis-matched as I would have been in a game with him. And now he knew it. His hands, his artist's hands tightened as Wilson drew on the cigarette. Smoke rose from the glowing coal — and within, a soul flickered near the balance. George stared at Wilson as a man might stare at himself in the mirror.

And then George smiled. His face and hands and body relaxed. He served and shrugged as the slam came past him again. 18-10. George served again. Wilson put it away. 19-10. It was a firing squad now and the audience was not pleased. George continued to smile. He served his last serve of the game. Wilson cuffed at it playfully, setting it up high for George to slam. George slammed and Wilson, ready, drilled the slam back into George's paddle which had hung briefly over the table. 20-10.

The last had been deliberate humiliation and George laughed easily, amused, as he tossed the ball to Wilson. Wilson had one last chance. He smiled and set himself to serve. Then, in the most spectacular breach of taste I have ever witnessed, in the most perfect precise machine-like execution of flair I have ever seen, Wilson passed the ball behind his back — the gun twirl of the professional — and, crouching low in the same motion, delivered George's own special serve — the defensive serve that spins just past the net and curls away off the table. Had George been ready for this serve, he could not have touched it; back two yards, awaiting the top-spin, he did not even move. Point and Game. 21-10.

George placed his hands upon the table, tired and smiling. He executed a brief bow and said: "There's not much point to another game. I'm beaten."

Wilson looked at him and his shoulders drew together. I think there was not a person in the room who did not for a moment understand the stakes of the game — the reason for Wilson's coming, and his failure. It was a tableau, and the rest of us framed it in silence. Then, slowly, people began to drift toward the other room again, and talk, and laugh, and forget the savage truth they had briefly known.

Footnote

Thus ends my promised epic. And I wonder if you understand it as dimly as I do yet. But my own story has a footnote:

I went to George. He was no longer smiling. His eyes were glazed, his mind was distant. "He used to hang out at the table-tennis club on 96th St." he murmured. "He spent allowance buying time to play us. That was years ago."

"Was that him?" I found myself saying, "Was that Wilson—the Wilson"?

"Yes," said George, "that was Wilson...and he was fast...."

His eyes focused. Karen came past and touched his arm. He smiled at her. She looked at me. There were tears in her eyes. We did not speak. She left the room and went out into the rain.

"How did you get so wet?" said George.

"Well...." I looked past the people I knew. Alvin was coming toward us.

"He's leaving." said Alvin. "He's going away."

I was afraid he was going to start crying. "Come back, Wilson."

"Of course." I said. "He's done." I looked at George. "I thought he almost had you."

"Almost." Said George.

"Look—" I said, "I'm really sorry you...lost...and I'm sorry you slept with Karen...but...I don't hate you for it...I...."

"I'm sorry, too. If I'd known...what it would do.... It was nice...it was a wonderful thing for me."

"Yes...I...." But my head was jerking like a yo-yo. And tears were pouring across my face like melting snow. And I was turning, my hands shaking before my face, twitching at obstacles I could not see. And I was running toward the exhibition room. Someone blocked me at the door, saying, "Here's that nickel I owe you." And I brushed past him into the crowd of the other room. And I stood swaying at the center under the shadow of the banner which read:

> *We neither drink*
>
> *Nor smoke*
>
> *Nor swear*
>
> *Norfolk.*

There were a million people facing me. And one was Julie the cellist, who was nervously chewing on her wrist-corsage. And I stood there facing them all. And I screamed. And then, in the last few moments before I collapsed with pneumonia that would condemn me to an army hospital for three months, in those last moments, my voice charged with energies I would never replace—I called out to them all:

"Come on, everybody, sing. It's easy—follow the bouncing ball...."

And I sang to them, though no one joined me. And I wonder now if you, my lords of truth, would care to sing along:

> *I'm an educated man*
>
> *To get more sense within my head I plan*
>
> *(dum dum dum dum dum dum)*
>
> *Well I've been on earth so long*
>
> *And I used to sing a little song*
>
> *While all those old timers took their stand.*

It is, you see, so very easy. You just follow the bouncing ball. One more time:

> *I'm an educated man*
>
> *To get more sense within my head I plan....*

.

www.ingramcontent.com/pod-product-compliance
Lightning Source LLC
Chambersburg PA
CBHW071252130626
46556CB00003B/1282